# *The* LIBERATION *of* GABRIEL KING

## K. L. GOING

**SCHOLASTIC INC.**
New York Toronto London Auckland Sydney
Mexico City New Delhi Hong Kong Buenos Aires

**liberate** *(li-bə-rāt) v.—*to set free;
release from control


This book is dedicated to my parents,
**WILLIAM AND LINDA GOING**,
who gave me a beautiful childhood
and the perspective to be grateful . . .

. . . and to **MARGERY FREEMAN**,
who called me a warrior. I wield my little plastic pen.

And to the
**ST. THOMAS COMMUNITY
OF NEW ORLEANS, LOUISIANA.**
Your spirit lives on through the lessons you taught.

ISBN-13: 978-0-545-02945-2
ISBN-10: 0-545-02945-7

12 11 10 9 8 7 6 5 4 3 2 1          7 8 9 10 11 12/0
Printed in the U.S.A.                    40

First Scholastic printing, January 2008
Design by Gina DiMassi
Text set in Bookman Light

# CONTENTS

# Chapter 1

# UNDER THE PICNIC TABLE

My best friend, Frita Wilson, once told me that some people were born chicken.

"Ain't nothing gonna make them brave," she'd said. "But others, they just need a little liberatin', that's all." Least that's how Frita told it.

If you'd asked me before the summer of 1976, I would have told you I was one of the chicken ones. If you could count on anything, it was that I, Gabriel Allen King, didn't do anything scary. I didn't climb out too far on the branches of the pecan trees or ride my bike on the same dirt road the truckers used. I didn't pick up ugly-looking bugs that might have pinchers or walk too close to the cotton fields if anyone even hinted that the cows might be loose. Most of all, I didn't intend on going to the fifth grade, ever.

But things don't always work out the way you plan, and what I didn't count on was Frita. I didn't expect she'd decide I was one of the ones needed liberatin', or that the best way to do it would be to overcome all our fears. I didn't expect a lot of things, and I guess if I'm going to tell you about them, I best start at the beginning.

It was the morning of our fourth-grade Moving-Up Day, and me and Frita were under the picnic table beside the elementary school. That's where we used to hide out during recess so nobody could find us. Only today wasn't a school day. It was a graduation day.

We could hear all the noise coming from the school yard just around the corner. Hollowell Elementary ain't that big, but the yard was packed with a stage, rows of folding chairs, extra-tall bleachers we used for special occasions, and lots of folks who were crowding in. But all that commotion was a distant buzz because me and Frita were lying on our backs in the shade, listing all the things that made the day great.

"Number one," Frita said, "today is a momentous occasion."

Frita liked to use big words like that. Most of the time I could figure them out by how she was talking, but other times I just pretended to know. I said, "Mmm-hmm. *Mooo-men-tus.*"

"We're fourth-grade graduates," Frita said. "That's pretty great."

"Yup," I agreed, "because now we've got no more school for the whole summer."

Frita pretended to write NO SCHOOL on the bottom of the picnic table. Then she took a big bite of a chocolate sprinkly cookie she'd gotten from the party table. The cookie crumbled all over her chin, but you could hardly notice. Frita's got dark chocolate skin, so the cookie crumbs blended right in.

"Starting today," Frita said with her mouth full, "we'll be upperclassmen. No more East Wing with the babies. We'll be West Wing fifth-graders."

Frita pretended to write WEST WING on the bottom of the picnic table, but I made an imaginary line through it.

"Now, why'd you go and cross that off?" Frita asked, pretending to write it back on again. Then she gave me that look she saved for when she was trying to be all innocent. Frita knew dang well that moving to the West Wing wasn't on my list of great things.

"You're going to love it," she told me. "You'll see. We'll have our own playing field and we won't have to eat in the cafeteria with the kindergarteners. We'll have outside gym every day—"

"Yeah," I said. "Outside gym with the *sixth-graders*. Cafeteria time with the sixth-graders and recess with the sixth-graders."

Sixth-graders meant Duke Evans and Frankie Carmen. I'd had a whole year free from torment since they'd moved to the West Wing ahead of us, but one year was definitely not enough.

"All the teachers in the West Wing are super mean," I added, settling myself into being stubborn. "Everybody says it, so you know it's true. *And* I'll be the shortest kid there."

"I won't let anyone get you," Frita told me, real solemn.

"Besides, fifth grade is a whole summer away. Maybe you'll grow taller by then."

I figured there was as much chance of me growing an entire foot over the summer as there was of snow in Georgia in June.

"Maybe," I said.

Frita grinned. "It'll be great," she said. "You'll see." Then she sat up. "Hey, I thought up numbers three and four for our list of great things. Graduation certificates and class pictures. Where do you think I should hang my picture? Above my bed, next to the mirror, or over the dresser?"

Frita'd been thinking about this ever since she got a picture frame with smiley faces on it for her birthday.

"You can hang yours up too, and then we'll match," she told me.

"Except I don't have a picture frame, and there's no way Momma can buy me one after she already bought me this outfit for Moving-Up Day. Sure would've rather had the picture frame."

Frita shrugged. "Then we'll just have to make you one. That'll be number five—starting today, we'll do projects all summer."

"And go swimming in the catfish pond . . ."

"And sleep in your tent . . ."

"And race our bikes . . ."

Frita looked at me.

"Gabe," she said, "I'm glad we're friends. Good thing Daddy made me do the integrating."

Integrating was one word I knew the meaning of. Frita'd said it lots of times and I used to think it meant visiting. Turns out it really means to make something whole again. Putting the parts back together. That made pretty good sense because before the Wilsons moved here, there was a Frita-sized hole right next to me.

"Wish we could sit next to each other at the ceremony," I said. "But I'll whistle extra loud when you get your certificate. I'll cheer enough for ten other people and I'll stand up and wave so you can see me from the stage."

"Promise?" Frita asked.

"Promise."

Frita stuck out her pinky and linked it with mine. We didn't say nothing, but I reckon Frita was thinking the same thing I was. *Sure was perfect down here.* I could've stayed there forever, only right then we heard our teacher, Ms. Murray, calling people to line up.

*"Tyler Zach, Andrew Womack, Frita Wilson . . ."*

Frita handed me the last sprinkly cookie—the one with the most sprinkles.

"See you later," she said, ducking out from under the picnic table.

"See ya," I said, then I whistled one of my super-duper whistles so she'd hear just how loud I could be when I wanted. Frita turned back one more time and grinned before taking off in a cloud of dust.

I lay back and thought how this was going to be the best summer ever. This was the year of the Bicentennial—the 200th birthday of the United States of America—and our very own governor, Jimmy Carter, was running for president. That meant there'd be parties, parades, and rallies. Not to mention the hugest fireworks we'd ever seen on the Fourth of July. The way I figured it, if me and Frita made a list of all the great things about the summer of 1976, it would be full to overflowing.

At least, that's what I thought.

# Chapter 2

# WAYLAID

SOMETIMES, LIFE HAS A WAY OF WAYLAYING THINGS. I WAS SITTING there under the picnic table, waiting for my name to be called, about to eat the last, best sprinkly cookie, when suddenly two sets of feet were scratching at the dust and life went from perfect to perfectly rotten in thirty seconds flat.

"If it ain't little Gabriel King."

It was Duke Evans, the biggest, meanest, most rotten fifth-grader ever. Only he was about to become a sixth-grader with a certificate to prove it, and as Frita said, that made him certifiably worse.

"What grade you going into next year? Kindergarten?" That was Frankie Carmen—Duke's best buddy.

"Nah," Duke said. "He's going to be with us next year. Ain't that right, Gabe?"

I started to sweat and it wasn't 'cause of the heat. I looked for the perfect hole to slip through so I could run and get Frita or my pop, but Duke stuck his head under the table and smiled at me upside down. He had hair like yellow straw, beady brown eyes, and two missing front teeth from fighting. When he smiled, it was like being smiled at by a crazy scarecrow on Halloween.

*"Lisa Lawrence, Ann Marie Kudrow, Gabriel King . . ."*

In the distance I heard Ms. Murray calling my name so I tried to crawl out, but I didn't get very far.

"Where do you think you're going?"

"Nowhere," I said, but my voice cracked.

"Did we tell you to talk?"

"No. I mean, yes. I mean . . . I got to line up. Maybe we better get back."

"Did you just tell us what to do?" Duke snarled.

I answered so quick, I choked on my spit. "No. Nope."

"Seems to me," Duke said, "you used to carry our lunch trays . . ."

"And clean up our stuff after gym class . . ."

"And don't forget how much you loved giving us those snacks your momma packed for you. In fact, I think you want to give me that snack right there."

Duke grabbed the sprinkly cookie from my hand. I'd forgotten I was holding it, and it was all smooshed up from me clutching it so tight, but Duke chomped it down quicker than a hungry mutt with a steak. Duke was *always* hungry.

"You can have all my snacks," I said, real quick. "I'll get you more after the ceremony too. Promise. Only I better go because they're playing the starting music and my momma and pop will be waiting. I've got to clap for Frita, and . . ."

Soon as those words were out of my mouth, I wished I

could stuff 'em back in. Right away Duke got that look in his eye. He stuck one finger into my chest real hard.

"You can go when I say so," he growled. "And I don't say so, because no one's going to clap for Frita Wilson if I can help it."

If Frita were here, Duke wouldn't have had the guts to say that. I should have made a run for it only I was too scared, and before I knew it, Frankie grabbed my arms and Duke grabbed my feet. Then Frankie pulled my arms out of my shirtsleeves, yanked the sleeves behind me, and tied them in a knot so tight I couldn't move a muscle.

"Let's see you try to clap for your girlfriend now," he said, leaning in until his face was right next to mine. He laughed like that was *sooo* funny and shoved me to the ground.

I landed on my butt in a puff of red dust.

"See you next year," Duke said, syrupy sweet.

I sat there watching their feet get smaller and smaller.

There's nothing worse than watching someone else's feet run to where you ought to be.

I pulled hard at my shirtsleeves, but that knot wouldn't budge. I thought about getting up and running over to the crowd, but the idea of it made my cheeks turn bright red with embarrassment. Plus what if Duke and Frankie were waiting for me?

I could hear the ceremony starting and everyone clapping. The principal was making his speech about what a fine year it had been at Hollowell Elementary. He called out the names for everyone to get their certificates. First the kinder-garteners, then the first-, second-, and third-graders, and then he was calling out the names for my class.

*"Miranda Tuttle, Frita Wilson . . ."*

The principal called Frita's name in the distance and I whistled and hollered loud as I could, just like I'd promised, but I knew no one could hear me.

That's when I gave up and shuffled under the picnic table in shame. I thought of the imaginary list me and Frita had made, and in my mind I crossed off everything. This wasn't a great day *or* a momentous occasion. It was the worst day. I'd broken my pinky swear to Frita. I'd never done that before. Not even once.

I thought about Duke and Frankie, and then I thought about my best friend walking across the stage, listening for my extra-loud whistle. That about killed me. If this was what the fifth grade had in store for me, I didn't think I could stand it. There were some things in life a man could not be forced to endure, and it was looking like fifth grade was going to be one of them.

# Chapter 3

# A PUNCH IN THE NOSE

ONCE FRITA FOUND ME UNDER THE PICNIC TABLE, SHE KNEW EXACTLY
what had happened.

"Did Duke Evans and Frankie Carmen do this to you?"
she asked, setting down her certificate and class picture so
she could untie my shirtsleeves.

"Yup," I said.

Frita shook her head. "I knew I should've come looking
for you as soon as you didn't line up, but Ms. Murray said,
'Don't you move, Frita Wilson,' and I thought for sure you'd
show up. . . . But don't worry, Gabe. I'm going to liberate you
from this situation and then we're gonna take care of business. Just you wait."

Liberate was a word I should have known because Frita'd
said it before, but right then I couldn't think of what exactly
it meant. Only from the look on Frita's face I guessed it
meant trouble.

"I can't believe they made you miss Moving-Up Day," Frita
said, her eyes burning like hot coals.

"Don't matter," I told her. "I'm not moving up anyway. I
decided it."

It was as if a cloud passed over Frita's face. She looked at me and her brow scrunched into a V.

"What do you mean you're not moving up?" she said. "They called your name, so you've got to."

"Nope," I said. "I made up my mind."

Frita frowned.

"You can't stay behind," she said. "We got to be in the same grade—otherwise, who will you play with? Won't be anyone to pass notes with, or to pick each other for teams. Who will help you with your math and who'll eat my brussels sprouts on chicken and biscuits day?"

I thought it over. Frita did have a point. Back before the integrating, life sure had been plain. A teacher had even written on my report card in kindergarten: *Gabe seems lonely and needs to make some friends.* I couldn't go to school without Frita.

"Why don't you stay back with me?" I suggested, but Frita wrinkled her nose and pretended like I hadn't said that.

"You'll love the fifth grade. Just try it," she said instead, using her whiniest, most pleading voice.

But I thought about Duke and Frankie and I knew Frita was wrong. I'd broken my pinky swear because of them.

I shook my head. "Nope," I said. "I'll just get beat up on every day, so I might as well stay back. I'd rather be alive in the fourth grade than dead in the fifth."

Frita stomped her foot. "They won't get you," she said. "I promise."

"Oh, yeah?" I asked. "How you going to promise that? You'd have to pay them all the money in the world . . ."

Frita stuck her stuff under one arm and grabbed my elbow.

"No, I won't," she said. "C'mon."

My stomach twisted into a knot. "What are you going to do? Are you going to tell Ms. Murray? Don't you think we should find my pop first?"

But Frita wasn't listening. Sometimes she's like a locomotive—there's no stopping her until she wants to be stopped. She dragged me to where the punch and cookies were set up and it didn't make a lick of difference that I was trying to run the other way.

"I'm going to do what Terrance taught me," Frita said. "And don't worry about getting in trouble—this is *justified* on account of what they did to you."

Justified? I wondered if justified was anything like terrified. Probably was if it was something Frita had learned from her older brother. Terrance was eighteen, and when it came to pounding, he was the expert. He kept five different punching bags in the basement of their house. There were big ones as tall as he was, tiny ones the size of someone's head, and there was one in the corner that was exactly my size.

One time me and Frita snuck down there when we thought no one was home. Only then we'd heard Terrance's feet coming down the steps—*clunk, clunk, clunk*. He didn't see us at first and started punching that little bag a hundred times a second. I breathed in real sharp by accident and that's when he turned around and saw us under the stairwell. First I screamed, then Frita screamed. Then Terrance chased us clean out of the house. I hadn't gone into her basement since.

So if Frita was going to pull something she'd learned from Terrance that could only mean one thing. Trouble.

"You know my momma will be wondering where I am," I said, right quick. "We better find her before we do anything else . . ."

I searched the crowd, but right then Frita caught sight of Duke, and that's when things got crazy.

"Just see if anyone picks on you again after this," Frita said.

She let go of my arm, marched straight up to Duke, drew back her fist, and before anyone could take a breath she punched him smack in the nose. Duke toppled back, knocking over the punch bowl, and Frita dove after him. She was rearing back to punch him again when Frankie tackled her from the side. All around me people were gathering in, pushing and yelling, but I was frozen solid.

*"Fight! Fight!"*

*"Get her . . ."*

*"You kids stop that!"*

Everything was happening at once, and before I could blink, there was a slew of adults pulling everyone apart and my pop was one of them. He dragged Frita off Duke, but it took two other guys to help because she kept swinging her arms like cyclones. Duke got to his feet and stood next to his pop. His nose was dripping blood and his clothes were all soaked in fruit punch and he was sniffling real hard, like he was trying not to cry.

Then his pop yelled, "You got beat up by a nigger girl?"

The whole crowd went silent soon as he said that. Even Frita stopped swinging and her eyes popped. My breath came out like someone had punched me in the gut, and I looked around to see who would yell at Mr. Evans for saying that, but all the adults were looking at the ground, shuffling their feet.

Then Pop stepped up.

"You best not be using that word," Pop said. He said it steady and quiet, like he says just about everything, but I could tell he meant business.

"You talking to me?" Mr. Evans asked, looking down. Pop is short like me—he's shorter than all the other adults—but he didn't back away.

"Yes, I am."

Mr. Evans moved like he might put up his fists, but he looked around at all the faces in the crowd and then he spat on the ground instead. It was hot and dry, so that spit sat at Pop's feet like a challenge. Then Mr. Evans grabbed Duke by the elbow.

"Come on," he said, real gruff.

He nodded into the crowd to Frankie's pop and they took

off. Our teacher, Ms. Murray, was trying to say something to them about their boys fighting, but they didn't even stop to listen. Only Duke stopped long enough to look back over his shoulder. His eyes narrowed into tiny slits, and there was so much hate in them, I could read exactly what his mind was saying.

*I'm gonna get you. Just you wait.*

# Chapter 4

# TEN TIMES WORSE

I KNOW FRITA WAS TRYING TO HELP, BUT REALLY SHE'D MADE THINGS ten times worse. I'd be a dead man if I went to the fifth grade now. Might as well call me a walking corpse.

Frita stared after Mr. Evans and I'd never seen such a strange expression on her face. Looked like she'd seen a ghost.

Pop dusted off her dress. "You okay?" he asked.

Frita looked back one more time, then she shrugged and looked real tough again. "I could have taken them if you adults hadn't interfered," she said.

Pop chuckled. "I suspect you could have."

"No suspect about it," Frita muttered, but she said it low, so maybe just I heard.

Pop reached down and picked up Frita's certificate and class picture from the dust. They were all trampled, and you could see where there was a hole right in the center of the picture.

He handed it back to Frita and she tried to look like it was no big deal, but her tough look faded again and her lower lip quivered just a little bit. I was going to say she could have mine soon as I got it, but that's when our teacher came over.

"I need to speak to your parents about you fighting, Frita Wilson," Ms. Murray said. "Is your father here this morning?"

"Yes, ma'am," Frita said, brushing a line of dirt off her certificate. "He's probably around by the stage, talking to people."

Frita's daddy was always talking to people—partly because he was a preacher, so folks felt inclined to tell him their troubles, and partly because he was involved in politics, so folks felt inclined to tell him the answers to other people's troubles. Least that's what Frita's momma said.

Ms. Murray shook her head. "Guess we'll have to go find him then, won't we?" She tried to look mad, but it was no secret Ms. Murray liked Frita a whole lot, so really she just sighed.

"Yes, ma'am," Frita said, kicking at a pebble. She turned to me. "Guess I better go."

"Yup," I said. "Guess so."

I wanted to say thanks for the liberatin' and all, even if she *had* made things worse, but Frita took off behind Ms. Murray and that left me and Pop.

"You want to tell me what happened?" Pop asked.

I looked down at my feet, but I didn't say anything. How do you explain to your pop that you got tied up under a picnic table?

"Your momma is not very happy about you missing the ceremony, and I don't blame her."

I shrugged. "Don't matter," I said, "because I'm not going to the fifth grade anyway."

Pop gave me that look that said I better not be a smart aleck, but I wasn't being smart, I was dead serious.

"And don't try to talk me out of it, because I've made up my mind."

Pop looked like he might try to talk me out of it anyway, but he didn't have a chance because that's when Momma caught up to us and it was like getting caught up to by a tornado. Her hands were on her hips, her blond hair was flying out of its ponytail, and she was coming up fast.

"Made up your mind about what?" she said.

"Fifth grade," I said. "I ain't going."

"Oh, is that what you think?" Momma asked, only she wasn't really asking because she didn't wait for an answer. Her hands shot up to her mouth. "What happened to your pants?"

I looked behind me and sure enough, there was red clay all over my butt. Probably from being pushed onto the ground by Duke.

"Did Frita Wilson put you up to this?" Momma asked. "Was she the one who was fighting?"

"No," I said, super quick. Then I said, "Well, yes," but Momma didn't seem to be listening.

"Your father took overtime down at the peanut mill so I could buy you those pants, and no one even got to see you wear them. When the principal called your name I'd never been so proud in my entire life, and then . . ."

Tears started to leak out of Momma's eyes. My eyes were starting to leak now too, on account of how the day had turned into such a mess. Pop looked at both of us and took a deep breath.

"Let's talk about this at home," he said.

Momma didn't say a word the whole ride back to the trailer park where we live, but when we got inside, she said, "Take off those pants right now so I can wash them."

She said it real cold, so I said, "Fine."

Pop set his truck keys on the counter and shook his head.

"I suspect Gabe feels bad, darlin'," Pop said, and he was right. Bad didn't begin to cover it.

"Well, good," said Momma. "He can feel bad straight through until next year. Straight through until he goes to the fifth grade and that's that."

She was half crying and half mad, and that made me feel just about the same.

"I won't do it!" I said, and then I burst into tears. Frita says I'm a crybaby, but I can't help it. Soon as I get upset, the waterworks turn on and there's no shutting them off.

"You will!" said Momma.

"Enough," said Pop, standing between us. "Gabe, go to your room so your momma and I can talk."

I knew they were going to talk about me, and that felt like being caught red-handed. "Fine," I said. "I won't ever come out. Especially not for the fifth grade."

Pop gave me that look that said, *Not another word,* so I stomped through the kitchen to my bedroom. I slammed the door shut and tore off my pants, then I pulled on my oldest, dirtiest overalls. I flung myself facedown on the bed and gave it up for good.

Terrance called me a wimp once because he says boys aren't supposed to cry, but Frita doesn't mind and Momma doesn't mind and usually Pop doesn't say nothing either. I heaved and coughed until my pillow got all wet and all the bad stuff came out through my nose.

I thought about Momma and Frita and how I'd disappointed them. Then I thought about Duke and Frankie and how it was all their fault. Part of me wanted to go back out and tell Momma and Pop what had really happened, but if I told Momma, she was sure to call Mr. Evans and Mr. Carmen and then Duke and Frankie would have even more reason to kill me. What was a man to do?

Life was grim. The future did not look good, and let me tell you, it was pressing in.

## Chapter 5

# AT THE CATFISH POND

Just about the moment I'd decided to run away from home and change my name so no one would ever find me, there was a knock on my door.

"Gabe," Pop said, "we're going for a walk."

Pop didn't wait for me to say yes or no. He just turned and headed toward the door. We live in the smallest trailer in the Hollowell Trailer Park, so he didn't have to go far. The inside is tight, but Momma decorated it nice with orange curtains and thick brown carpet. The outside paint is flaking off the shutters, and Pop always says he's going to fix that someday, but he never does. When I got outside, Pop was chipping away some dirty brown paint with his finger, but he stopped when I walked out.

"Let's go," he said.

Georgia is mighty hot in the summer when the sun is high and there ain't no clouds, so Pop and I walked real slow. I knew we were headed toward the catfish pond because that's the only place anyone headed when it was hot like this. But first you had to walk to the far end of the trailer park, and that meant going past the Evans trailer.

I might live in the smallest trailer in the Hollowell Trailer Park, but Duke Evans lived in the scariest. It was all torn apart, with boards hanging off the windows and parts of cars all over the front yard. Plus, no one knew for certain if Duke's momma was alive or not. Erin Morgan said she was perfectly fine and mean as a whip, but Duane Patterson said you could smell her corpse when the wind was right.

I sniffed at the air as we got closer and sure enough, I thought I caught a whiff.

"Let's cut through over here," I said to Pop. He gave me a look, but he didn't say nothing, so we took the secret path me and Frita had cut out behind one of the other trailers. I kept looking back over my shoulder though, and picked up the pace.

Me and Pop crossed the old dirt road and walked through the tall pine trees toward the cotton field. We stepped across the line where the stretched-out shadows of the pine trees reached over the cotton field. Pop's big old work boots snapped the brown stalks and the white cotton balls before we crossed into the woods.

Pop put one rough hand on my head.

"I suspect it wasn't entirely your fault that you missed Moving-Up Day," he said. "I know you didn't mean to hurt your momma's feelings." He paused. "The thing is, you haven't got much choice about the fifth grade. Sometimes we've got to do things whether we like them or not. Understand?"

I nodded, but I was still thinking about Duke and his pop.

"Pop?" I said.

"Mmm?"

"How come Mr. Evans called Frita that name?"

I was used to kids at school calling Frita names when she wasn't around to punch their lights out, but they called me names too—like Shrimp and Shorty. I'd always figured that was just about the same thing. Only there sure weren't any adults calling me Shrimp.

Pop thought things over.

"Well," he said at last, "some folks don't care for black people."

"How come?" I asked.

Pop frowned. "Don't know for certain. I suspect they see the world as having only so much of the good things in life, and they're afraid of sharing because then there will be less for them. That other person might get something they want."

"Is that true?" I asked.

"No," said Pop. "That's not how I see it. I suspect there's enough good to go around."

We walked real quiet again until we reached the pond. It was deserted today and I was glad there weren't any sixth-graders hanging out by the rope swing to yell things at me when my pop was around. Since the coast was clear, I sat right under the big old cypress tree, where the edge dropped down, and slipped off my sneakers so I could dunk in my feet. The water was muddy and warm.

Pop didn't take off his work boots, but he knelt down and

stuck one hand in. He stared for a long time, like he was thinking what to say next.

"Gabe," he said after a little while, "you and Frita have to watch yourselves. You know that, right?"

I wasn't sure exactly what Pop meant, but I had an idea—like when Frita used big words. Made my stomach feel funny. Pop studied me careful.

"I'm not telling you to fight, but sometimes a person has to stand up for himself. You can't live your life being afraid of boys like Duke."

I didn't say anything—just swished my feet around.

"Your momma was some disappointed not to see you walk across that stage today. Now you'll never have another chance. I know there were reasons you didn't make it, but you got to think to yourself . . . Do I want to let someone take something from me that I can never get back again?"

I stopped swishing.

"Like Moving-Up Day?"

Pop nodded.

"And the fifth grade?"

He nodded again. "You think things over," he told me, "and I'll go back and talk with your momma. When you're ready, you come home and tell her you're sorry. All right?"

I looked around the empty pond. What if the sixth-graders showed up? What if Duke was with them?

"I'll go home with you, Pop," I said, but Pop shook his head.

"You're fine," he told me, but what he meant was, *You're staying put until you figure some things out.*

"Yes, sir," I said, but I said it extra miserable so he might change his mind.

Pop reached over and ruffled my hair. He stood up, then headed back the way we'd come. I watched him get smaller and smaller. Long as he was in sight, things felt okay, but the minute he disappeared, the world shrank in. All the trees got closer and the cypress roots looked like giant tentacles reaching up to grab me. The rope swing hung like a gallows, and without meaning to, my mind pictured what it would feel like to swing through the air, then plunge far below, turning over and over in the muddy water.

Everything I'd eaten churned in my stomach until I thought I might be sick. I heard a snap and thought for sure it was either an alligator or a sixth-grader sneaking up on me, and I sure as heck wanted to light out of there.

But then I thought over what Pop had said about not letting people take stuff from me. Maybe he meant something like this, a summer afternoon when I had the whole catfish pond to myself. But how could I just decide not to let other people take things? Seemed to me I was too chicken to stop 'em.

Now how was I going to change that?

# Chapter 6

# INTO TOWN

A MAN CAN DO A LOT OF THINKING AND STILL COME TO THE SAME CON-
clusion. Best to stay put where life is decent. Of course, Frita
still hadn't offered to stay behind with me, but I guessed
she'd come around once she discovered how serious I was
about staying back. I figured I'd ask her again eventually,
but eventually snuck up on me real quick.

It was a Tuesday morning, and me and Frita were making a track and field course outside my trailer.

"Let's pretend we're in the Olympics," Frita said. The
Olympics were coming up and Frita had been reading all
about them.

"This part of the road can be the track and then we can
bring out stuff to be the hurdles and the high jump."

We looked around the trailer until we found what we
needed. There was a lamp with a broken switch, Momma's
old blender that wouldn't blend, the pillows from the couch
with the stuffing falling out, the stool with the cracked seat
cover, and three buckets.

"Someone's got to count," Frita said, "so we know if we set
any world records."

I said I'd count first, so Frita lined up beside the lamp.

"On your mark, get set . . ."

The mailman walked right into our course and tripped over the blender. "Crazy kids," he said, shaking his head. He took out a yellow slip and handed it to me. "This one's for you, Gabe. Guess you've got a package down at the post office."

The mailman put the rest of the mail in the box, then headed next door. Frita ran up to see my package slip, but she jumped over all the obstacles first, ending with a flying leap onto the pillows. I counted and she made it in record time. Record for Hollowell, Georgia, anyway.

She stood up and hopped over to me. "Did you order something?" she asked when she reached me.

"Nope," I said. "Maybe it's for Pop."

"But it says it's for you," Frita pointed out. "Ask your momma if we can walk into town and get it."

Frita reached down and scooped up a huge daddy longlegs that was crawling over the finish line. She dangled him between her thumb and forefinger and I jumped a mile even though that spider wasn't anywhere near me. I ran right quick to the trailer and poked my head inside the front door.

"Momma," I yelled, "can me and Frita walk into town?"

All I heard was a muffled sound from the back, but that was yes enough for me.

"Okay, we're going!" I hollered.

I went back out to the yard where Frita was setting that spider down on the pillows real careful.

"Ready?" I asked, keeping my distance.

The daddy longlegs scampered away. *Good riddance.*

"Yup," Frita said. "Let's take the old dirt road. It's quicker."

I felt my gooseflesh rising.

The old dirt road was a narrow stretch between the peanut mill and the town of Hollowell, and nobody used it except the eighteen-wheelers that came to pick up the peanuts. They came barreling down out of nowhere. Momma always said a man could get run over and killed on a stretch of road like this and no one would know it for days. Me and Frita talked about it once and we guessed you'd get eaten by buzzards. They'd pick at you with their huge beaks until you were nothing but a pile of bones.

"Who's in a rush?" I asked.

Frita said, "Don't be a chicken, Gabriel King."

Then she took off, so I didn't have any choice but to follow.

We left the obstacle course set up and ran through the trailer park, then cut through the secret path. Soon as we stepped onto the old dirt road, I looked up and down for eighteen-wheelers. Then I looked in the sky for buzzards, just in case, but there weren't any. There was only dry dust chokin' up my tongue and making it hard to breathe. Everything was pressing in again, even with Frita right there beside me.

"Race ya," I said, so we could get to town faster. I took off three seconds early and ran full out, but Frita still beat me by a mile. By the time I turned onto Main Street, she was already sitting in front of the post office. I could see her perfectly clear because there are only seven buildings in the town of Hollowell, so you can see just about everything at once. There's the post office, the town hall with its big green lawn and gazebo, Mae's Pit Stop Restaurant, the general store, the Baptist church, and the gas station. Then a little farther down there's the Hollowell Elementary School.

Frita stood up when she saw me coming.

"What took you so long?" she asked, but she didn't say it mean, only teasing. I was all winded, so I handed Frita my yellow slip and she marched up the steps into the post office and gave it to Mr. Alfred. I walked in real slow behind her, taking in big gulps of air.

"Morning, Frita. Morning, Gabe," Mr. Al said. He looked at me and shook his head, chuckling. "What are you two up to today?" he asked.

"Nothin', " Frita said.

Mr. Al went in the back and brought out a big manila envelope and handed it to me. I tore it open.

*This certifies that*
**GABRIEL ALLEN KING**
*completed the Fourth Grade*
*at Hollowell Elementary School*
*Hollowell, Georgia, May 1976.*

There was a class picture inside the envelope too. I frowned and stuffed everything back in.

"Something good?" Mr. Al asked.

"No," I said.

Me and Frita went outside and sat down on the lawn in front of the town hall. I picked a pebble out of the grass and threw it at one of the election posters hanging up on the community board. I aimed for the one of Gerald Ford and pretended he was Duke Evans. Then I pretended I was Jimmy Carter and everyone was going to vote over which one of us went to the West Wing next year because there sure wasn't room for both of us.

Me and Frita were quiet for a long time.

"At least you got a class picture," she said at last.

I pulled it out of the envelope and there I was, front and center, looking like a first-grader. My hair was all messed up, like a rat's nest. I'd forgotten it was picture day, so I'd worn my oldest tattered overalls. Frita was two rows above me and her hair looked perfect, all done up in a neat bun on top of her head. She was smiling real huge. There were only ten kids in our class, but even so, Frita stood out. She was the only black person in the picture and the only girl on the top row.

I remembered how Frita's class picture got all crushed in the dust, so I yawned like I was bored instead of grumpy.

"Who wants a stupid old picture anyway," I said. "Maybe I'll throw it away."

"Throw it away?" Frita said, opening her eyes wide. "You can't waste a good picture like this. Look, there's Ms. Murray—the best teacher we ever had. You want a picture of Ms. Murray, don't you?"

"Nah," I said. "You can have it. I'll get another one next year."

Frita took the picture out of my hands.

"Well, I'll keep it if you're going to throw it away," she said, "but you know you're not staying behind. You got a certificate to prove it, right there."

I picked up another pebble and aimed for Gerald Ford again, but this time I hit Jimmy Carter right on the nose. Frita shook her head.

"Gabe," she said, "we got to do something about you."

"You mean so I don't get pounded?"

"I mean so you'll move up with me next year."

"Why can't you stay behind?"

Frita wrinkled her nose.

"Then how would we ever get out of elementary school? Nope," she said. "We got to think of a plan."

"A plan?"

"Yup," said Frita. "Something to help you stop being chicken."

I scowled. Didn't seem to be anything that could do that, but I thought it over.

"Frita," I said at last.

"Yeah?"

"If we can't make me brave, *then* will you stay behind with me?"

Frita frowned, but finally she shrugged.

"I guess," she said. "But I'm going to come up with something, and when I do, you better try it. No halfsies. Deal?"

"Deal," I said, sticking out my pinky.

Frita linked hers with mine and we shook on it.

## Chapter 7

# FRITA'S PLAN

WHEN FRITA SAYS SHE'S GOING TO COME UP WITH A PLAN, YOU BETTER watch out, because it is by God going to happen. The very next day she called me on the phone to say she'd come up with an idea, so I rode my bike over to her house even though it was pouring down rain. Got there in ten minutes flat, but I was still soaked. Frita met me in the driveway and I could tell she was excited. Her eyes were sparkling like water in a puddle after the sun comes out.

"Here's what you're going to do," she said, as soon as I'd dried off and we were in her room with the door shut. "First, you're going to make a list. Write down everything you're afraid of." She narrowed her eyes until they were teeny, tiny slivers. "And you *better* be honest or it won't work."

"I've got to write down *everything*?"

Frita nodded. She handed me paper and a pencil and waited for me to write.

"Then what'll we do?" I asked, suspicious.

Frita grinned. "Then we'll cross 'em off one by one, saving Duke Evans and the fifth grade for last when you're most brave."

I about choked. *That was the plan?*

"Nuh-uh," I said, leaving that paper in a heap, but Frita gave me a look that could have withered okra on the stalk.

"You pinky-swore," she reminded me.

Drat.

I picked up the pencil and made a column of numbers down one side of the paper. I wrote *fifth grade* next to number one even though we were going to save that till last. Then I wrote down *Duke Evans, Frankie Carmen, spiders,* and *alligators* next to numbers two, three, four, and five.

"You done?" Frita asked after a while.

"Nope," I said.

Frita jumped on the bed. She was wearing a bright orange jumpsuit with flared ankles, and every time she jumped, the flares puffed around her legs.

"Done yet?"

I wasn't. I was only on number eighteen.

"Maybe I'd be able to finish if you'd let me concentrate . . ."

Frita was quiet for a long time. She did handstands against the wall and watched me upside down. I started a second column down the other side of the paper.

"*Now* are you done?" she finally asked.

Truth was, there were maybe just a few more things I could have written down, but I said yes just so she'd stop asking.

"Okay," said Frita, sliding against the wall. She crumpled

in an upside-down heap of gangly legs and elbow-y arms. "What's the first thing on your list?"

"You mean aside from Duke and Frankie and the fifth grade?"

Frita nodded.

"Spiders," I said slowly. Big ones, small ones, and hairy fanged ones. I'd never met a decent spider.

"Okay," said Frita, "we'll start with that."

"What are we going to do?" I asked, but Frita didn't answer. She took her raincoat out of her closet and pulled on her yellow galoshes.

"You'll see . . . ," she said. "This is the best plan ever."

Then she stopped.

"Better get the jars and flashlights out of the basement," she muttered.

I stopped dead in my tracks. Frita's basement was number eight on my list and she didn't even know it.

"I'll wait up here," I said, but Frita grabbed my arm.

"We're just going down for a minute," she told me. Then she walked out of her room and down the hall, dragging me with her. There was a light at the top of the basement stairs, but it was too high up even for Frita to reach, so we crept down the steps real slow. They creaked under our weight and Frita's feet made loud squishing sounds in her galoshes. I listened just in case Terrance was down there waiting for someone to pound on, but there wasn't a sound. Then I listened in case he was upstairs waiting to sneak up on us like he'd done when we were checking out his punching bags. But I didn't hear anything from that direction either.

My heart was beating super fast. *Ka-thump, ka-thump, ka-thump.*

It was dank and musty in the Wilsons' basement, and everywhere I turned, there were posters that said MALCOLM X on them and drawings of panther heads staring at me from the darkness. I turned in a full circle, staring at the walls, wondering why Terrance hung out down here. Mrs. Wilson said a boy his age needed privacy, but I didn't see what was so private about punching things.

I followed Frita away from the stairs over to a box that was sitting on the floor. She dug around for the flashlights while I stood next to the little punching bag, breathing in the smell of sweat. My eyes started to adjust and I studied the canvas real hard. That's when I saw it—even in the darkness.

There was blood on one corner.

I stepped back quick, my heart beating twice as fast, and backed right into Frita, who was putting new batteries into one of the flashlights.

"What's wrong?" she asked, but I could hardly breathe.

"Let's get out of here," I whispered.

"Why?" Frita said, taking out two jars and turning on the flashlight. "We're just getting the stuff we need. Isn't any reason why we shouldn't—"

That's when Frita's flashlight went out.

*"BOO!"*

I screamed, and then I saw him.

Terrance was standing right behind Frita, one hand over the front of her flashlight.

I didn't wait around. I took off so fast, I should have gotten a gold medal. There was a space the width of one small person between Terrance and the wall, and I squeezed through it and bolted up the stairs.

"Where you going, Twerp?" Terrance called out after me, but I was already gone. I hadn't even put my raincoat on, but I stood outside and got drenched waiting for Frita.

## Chapter 8

# SWAMP SPIDERS

Frita was some miffed.

"Stupid Terrance," she said. "I bet the basement was on your list and now you're twice as scared of it. Big brothers ruin everything," she muttered. We turned off onto the old dirt road. "But don't worry. We still got plenty more things to cross off."

That's what I was afraid of.

We walked a little farther, but I stuck close to Frita. The old dirt road was worse than ever on gloomy days like this, and I was jumpy as a flea. The roots of my hair were still standing on end.

"Maybe we should go back to my place . . . ," I said, but Frita gave me that look again.

"Gabriel King," she told me, "this is good practice. I bet a million dollars the old dirt road is on your list too, isn't it?"

"So?" I said.

Frita got that look in her eye.

She thought for a minute, then, before I knew it, she took off running. Just like that. I tried to catch up, but Frita was way faster than me and pretty soon I was all by myself.

"Frita?" I hollered.

There was no answer, so I stopped and stood in the middle of the road. It was silent and shadowy and the rain was making a mist, thick as pea soup.

"Frita?" I said again, only this time it came out as a croak.

Only there was no Frita.

I looked back over my shoulder, thinking I might head home again, but the way back looked just as creepy as the way forward. Shadows danced in both directions. *Truck shadows, cow shadows, and huge looming Terrance shadows.*

My muscles froze so I could barely move. I thought about calling for Pop, but I knew he would never hear me. Instead I took one step, then two steps . . . Then I heard it. Sounded like a freight train coming straight at me. First the deep roar of the engine, then the bellow of the horn. I turned and sure enough, there were two headlights coming closer and closer . . .

My eyes opened wide, but still I couldn't move an inch.

There was an eighteen-wheeler headed straight toward me. The horn sounded again, louder this time, and I tried to make my legs go, but I was stuck in place. One more minute and I'd be buzzard food for sure.

That's when something snapped. I sprung like a rubber band stretched too tight and dove into the ditch. The horn bellowed one more time, so loud I had to cover my ears with both hands. I lay flat and shut my eyes, but still I felt it in my stomach as the eighteen-wheeler roared by with a gust of wind and water.

After that, everything was silent. Everything except Frita, whooping in the distance.

"*Woo-hooo!* Wasn't that great?" she hollered from somewhere far away. "Did you hear that? You hear how he laid on that horn for us?"

Her voice was getting louder and louder as she ran toward me. I stood up and brushed myself off, but my legs were Jell-O and my heart was going really fast. I felt around in the grass until I found my jar and flashlight.

Frita caught up to me and skidded to a stop.

"Did you see the truck driver wave, Gabe?" she asked, dancing around in her yellow slicker. "That was the best."

Best wasn't exactly the word I'd have used to describe it, but Frita didn't care. She was all excited.

"Come on," she said. "Let's run super fast."

I wasn't sure my legs would move at all, let alone *super fast,* but Frita took off and I wasn't about to get left behind twice. I followed like a calf at her heels. She ran past the catfish pond and kept running until we'd reached the swampy area deep in the woods.

"You sure we should be back here?" I asked.

Frita waded into the muck. "Yup," she said. She pulled her flashlight out of her pocket. "It's perfect."

I didn't see what was so perfect about it. There's nothing

in a swamp but creepy old cypress trees with roots that stick up out of the ground, and Spanish moss that hangs down. There are slick snakes that slither by and spiderwebs with giant yellow-and-black spiders hanging in the middle. Plus, Terrance said there are corpses in the swamps. Corpses of kids half eaten by alligators.

Corpses and alligators were *both* on my list.

I tiptoed in, barely getting my feet wet, still thinking about the way that truck had barreled by.

"Frita?" I hollered. "Let's go home."

She was way ahead of me, shining her flashlight into the gray gloomy trees. I followed at a distance, and as I walked, my sneakers sunk deep into the muck. It had stopped raining now, but the trees were all drippy, and every now and then an extra-big drip would collect on the end of a clump of moss and wait there until I looked up so it could fall smack in my eye.

"You could at least tell me what we're looking for," I yelled, but Frita didn't answer, so I stuck the jar in the crook of an old bent tree and sat down on a dead branch.

It was quiet for a long time and I started to worry Frita'd been eaten, until I heard her hollering.

"Quick! Get the jar! Hurry!"

"What's the matter?"

"I found one! I found one!"

"Found what?"

"A spider!" Frita yelled. "Come quick!"

I'd been hurrying, but soon as she said that, I slowed way down.

*A spider?!*

Frita jumped up and down, waving her arms. Her yellow slicker had belonged to Terrance first, so it was too big for her and the arms looked like flags in the distance. I stalled for a long time so the spider could hightail it out of there. First, I pretended I couldn't remember where I'd put the jar. Then I walked real slow, like I was trying to avoid all the deep spots.

"The jar! The jar!" Frita yelled.

When I finally reached her, she was standing in front of a giant spiderweb that stretched the whole distance between two huge cypress trees. A human being could get caught and eaten in a web that big. I swallowed hard, hoping the spider had made its getaway, and Frita danced from one leg to the other.

"Quick! Give me the jar."

I paused real long. "You mean this jar?"

"Yes! Hurry!"

I studied the jar, thinking maybe it needed some polishing up before I could hand it over, but I didn't have a chance to do anything because Frita grabbed it out of my hands.

"I found the best spider," she said.

Now, in my book there was no such thing as a best spider. Maybe an invisible spider would be a best spider, but even that wouldn't be any good because I didn't want to think of invisible spiders crawling on me when I didn't know about it.

I squinted at the web. "I don't see any spider," I said, thinking it probably took the hint and scrammed, but that's when Frita pointed up. There, right above my head, was the biggest yellow-and-black spider I had ever seen. It was so big and fat, I wondered how it could stay on the web without falling through. Every last drop of blood drained from my face and rushed to my toes.

Frita was some excited. She reached toward the spider with the jar, but she could hardly stop fidgeting. She positioned the jar in back of the spider and the lid in front of the spider, and then she started to move real slow . . .

That's when I felt it on me. Spiders were famous for jumping long distances, and I could feel its hairy legs on my neck. I let loose a scream, and then I started shaking and twisting, trying to get it off. Frita was yelling and hollering too, but I couldn't stop to listen.

"It's on me," I yelled. "Get it off! Get it off!"

I imagined it slipping inside the neck of my shirt, so I tore that shirt off and peeled out of my overalls. I was dancing around in my underwear and sneakers, and all I could think about was getting out of that swamp and getting home once and for all. I ran fast as I could, yelling and splashing, and every step I took, I felt that spider on me. I ran so fast, I blazed a trail straight back to the trailer park.

I didn't stop moving until I reached my place. Then I flung

open the front door and ran straight past Momma into my bedroom, where I tore off my sneakers and underwear. I shook my whole body and watched for flinging spiders, but there weren't any. Then I stood in front of my mirror and looked real careful. I even checked my hair to make sure it hadn't hitched a ride in there.

Momma kept knocking on the door, saying she was going to come in, and when your momma says she's coming in, it's pretty much true even if you tell her you are naked and checking for huge man-eating spiders. I pulled a new pair of overalls out of my dresser and I was buttoning them up just as Momma opened the door.

"Gabriel King, what on earth were you doing running through the trailer in your underwear? What happened to your overalls and shirt?"

I shrugged. Truth was, I couldn't quite recall.

"Were you out in the woods with—"

Just like that, Frita appeared at the front door. She was carrying my overalls and trying hard not to laugh. Momma opened the front door and Frita walked in carrying the jar with the spider. She tried to hand the jar to me, but I wouldn't take it. Momma shook her head.

"I don't want to know," she said. "I just don't want to know."

That was a good call on Momma's part. She went back to the living room and once she was gone, I gave Frita a hard look.

"You better not tell another living soul . . . ," I started, but Frita wasn't laughing.

"I won't tell," she said. "I wouldn't even tell Terrance if he tortured me. You just got a little bit spooked is all." She handed me back my shirt and overalls, and I glanced at the spider.

"Did you get it after it fell off me?" I asked.

Frita paused for a long time. "Uh-huh," she said at last.

"Think we should kill it?"

Frita grabbed the jar and held it tight against her chest.

"We can't kill it," she said. "You've got to make friends with it. That's how you'll stop being scared of spiders."

Frita patted the jar like a puppy.

"You got to name him," she said. "Once you name him, you'll feel like he's yours and then you won't be scared of him anymore."

This was the worst plan I'd ever heard.

"Frita," I said, "I don't think this is such a . . ."

Frita handed me the jar and smiled the way her daddy smiled from the pulpit.

"Trust me," she said. "You just got to have faith."

# Chapter 9

# WATERGATE AND
# PEANUT FARMERS

FRITA SAID FAITH WAS BELIEVING IN WHAT YOU COULD NOT SEE, AND pressing on until you could see it. Well, I wasn't going to be pressing nowhere with any spider. In fact, I wasn't going to so much as look at that spider again no matter what Frita had planned. I wasn't going to name him, make him my pet, or anything. And I sure as heck wasn't going to overcome any more fears. I was sure of it. At least, I was sure of it until Jimmy Carter got in the way.

He came up on account of my having to take a bath before dinner because I smelled like swamp muck. My taking a bath meant Pop turned on the news soon as he got home because I wasn't ready for dinner yet. Most days, Pop and the news didn't mix because soon as he turned on the TV, he got all riled up. Sometimes it was the cost of gasoline that got under his skin, or them talking about what had happened in Vietnam, but most of the time it was the election.

When I got out of my bath, I could hear Walter Cronkite, the anchorman, reading the news, and by the time I put on my pajamas and climbed onto the couch, Pop was scowling something fierce.

"What's happening, Pop?" I asked, curling up next to him. Pop was still in his work clothes, so he smelled like peanuts and fertilizer.

"Darn election," he said. "Jimmy Carter's not doing so good. Gerald Ford moved ahead in the polls. You'd think people would want a change after everything we've been through."

I shrugged.

"Maybe they want things to stay the same," I said, but Pop gave me a look.

"Things can't stay the same forever," he told me. "Sometimes you've got to fight to make sure things *do* change."

Momma hollered from the kitchen. "Allen!" she said to Pop. "Don't get started. Gabe doesn't want to hear about politics."

But Momma was wrong. I did want to hear about politics.

"How come you don't like Gerald Ford?" I asked. "Because he's not from Georgia?"

"No," Pop said. He got up and turned off the TV. "You know what happened with Watergate?"

I shook my head. I sort of knew, but not exactly.

"Watergate," said Pop, "was the reason President Nixon had to resign. You see, the Nixon White House wasn't very honest from the beginning. First, the vice president had to quit because he did something sneaky with his taxes. Then President Nixon had to resign because he was caught ordering people to spy on the Democratic Party at the Water-gate Hotel."

"Wow," I said. I thought spying was pretty cool, but Pop shook his head.

"Spying is never a good thing," he said, "but it's especially bad when the president does it. He was going to use that information to hurt the Democratic campaign, and if he did that, how would people make good decisions about voting? Elections are supposed to be fair, and if they're not, then we're no different from any other country. The president is supposed to understand that."

Pop paused. "You know what's worse?" he asked. "After everyone found out what he'd done, President Nixon still lied about the whole thing, only they caught him on tape."

"Really?" I asked. "Did he get in trouble?"

I figured he went to jail, but Pop shook his head. "No," he said.

"What happened to him?"

"Well, the guy who took over as president—he promised everyone he wasn't going to do *anything* sneaky, only right away he let Mr. Nixon off the hook for everything. That's called a pardon." Pop leaned in. "You know who that man was?"

"Nope."

"That man was Gerald Ford."

My eyes about bugged out of my head. "The same Gerald Ford who's running against Jimmy Carter?"

"Yup," said Pop. He raised one eyebrow. "Still think things should stay the same?"

Sure was a lot more complicated than I'd thought.

"Besides," Pop told me, settling back on the couch, "even if Watergate hadn't happened, I'd still be voting for Carter. He's one of us. Used to be a peanut farmer. Did you know that?"

I sure didn't. "You mean a peanut farmer can run for president?"

Pop nodded, then he looked at me real steady. "You want to hear a story about Jimmy Carter?" he asked. I always wanted to hear a story when Pop was telling it, so I leaned in close and breathed in the smell of peanuts.

"Well," said Pop, "when Jimmy Carter was living in Plains, which is a town just about like Hollowell, he ran a peanut warehouse. This was before you were born and lots of stuff was changing between black folks and white folks. Some people weren't too happy about that. They wanted everything to stay the same."

Pop poked me in the stomach. "Some of the men in the South started a group called a White Citizens Council. The whole purpose of that group was to keep up the laws that kept black and white people separate."

"Segregation?" I asked. That was a word I'd heard Frita use plenty of times.

"That's right," said Pop. "They wanted to keep up segregation. So you know what they did? They tried to get every white man in Plains to join that council. They were bullies—like that kid at school . . ."

"Like Duke?" I said, sitting up.

"That's right," said Pop. "They wanted to bully Jimmy Carter into signing up for their group. They said if he didn't, they wouldn't buy from his warehouse anymore and his store would go out of business."

"What'd he do?" I asked, leaning forward. "Did he have to join up? Did he move to another state?"

Pop shook his head.

"No sir," he said. "He was the only white man in Plains not to join."

I sat back against the couch. *Huh.* I bet that took some courage.

"You know why he stood his ground?" Pop asked.

I shook my head.

"Because he had something he didn't want them to take from him. Integrity." Pop stood up and ruffled my hair. "Maybe you'll run for president someday," he said with a wink. "If you make it through the fifth grade."

Pop went into the kitchen and I sat on the couch, thinking. I sure could use some courage, and now that Pop mentioned it, maybe I could use some integrity too.

Maybe it wouldn't kill me to give Frita's plan one teeny, tiny try.

# Chapter 10

# A DARN GOOD NAME

AFTER THAT, I WENT OUT EACH NIGHT AND SAT ON THE FRONT STEPS TO watch the spider. He sure was ugly looking. I didn't think I could stand having one as a pet, but if I was going to get me any courage, there didn't seem to be a way around it. So, two days later, I finally called Frita on the phone and told her she should come over because I'd made up my mind. I was keeping the spider.

Frita couldn't come over that night because she had a meeting for the Rockford Baptist Peace Warriors. But on Saturday her daddy drove her over in their station wagon and she got out lugging an old fish tank that she'd dug out of her basement.

"Look," Frita said, showing me the tank as soon as she arrived. She lifted up the lid, then popped it back on again. "Your spider can live in here. It's perfect." She picked up the glass jar I was keeping him in and pressed her finger to the side so it looked like she was tickling the spider's stomach. "You're going to keep him for good, right?"

I stared at the spider's awful, ugly eyes.

"Looks like it," I said.

Frita twirled around in a circle. "It's working," she sang. "My super-duper plan is working."

I wasn't so sure, but I didn't have time to press the point because that's when Pop got home. Pop was working weekends so as to get us some extra money to buy a car. His old truck spattered and coughed as he turned into the driveway.

"Hey there, Frita," Pop said, climbing out. "Hey, Gabe." He walked over and kissed the top of my head. He was filthy from head to foot, but I didn't mind. "What are you two doing?" he asked.

Frita showed him my spider and the new tank. She put a layer of grass in the bottom, then stuck a couple sticks inside.

"Gabe's going to keep him as a pet," Frita said. "He's not scared of spiders anymore because he likes this one."

Like was an awful strong word.

Pop squinted at the spider. "Is that so?" he asked. "Well, what kind of spider is he?"

Me and Frita shrugged. We hadn't figured that part out yet.

"What are you feeding him?" Pop asked. "A spider needs food and water to live. And it's a good thing you've got him a nice new tank because that jar is too small to keep a spider that size in."

Pop sat down on the front step beside me and Frita and held the jar up to get a better look.

"Lee Ann, bring out the guidebook," he yelled to Momma, who was inside getting hot dogs ready for dinner. Pop had a whole series of guidebooks—one for birds, one for reptiles, and one for insects and spiders. He once said he might've gone to school to study stuff like that if he'd been a smart man, but he wasn't book smart, just hands smart. I thought Pop was just about every ways smart.

Momma brought out the guidebook. Plus, she had a tray full of hot dogs, ketchup, mustard, chili, soda pops, and a big glass of water with ice cubes. She set the tray down where the spider's jar had been, then she sat on the top step behind Pop and put her chin on his shoulder to get a better look.

"He's a beauty," Momma said.

How come even Momma thought this was a good-looking spider?

Pop found a couple pictures in the guidebook that weren't quite right, then he turned the page and there was our spider staring back at us.

"*Argiope aurantia*—the yellow garden spider," Pop read. "Says here, the yellow garden spider is found throughout the United States. The body of the female is three-fourths to one and one-eighth inches across and the body of the male is one-fourth to three-eighths inches across." Pop surveyed my spider. "I'd say you've got a male here. He's not too big."

Not too big? This was one gigantic spider, but I didn't argue.

"The yellow garden spider is diurnal—that means they're active in the daytime. And they're carnivorous. That means they eat meat."

Ha! I knew it.

"People?" I asked.

"Hot dogs?" Frita suggested, but Pop laughed.

"No," said Pop. "They eat insects—bees, wasps, and grasshoppers."

Now I was starting to lose my appetite.

I didn't think I could take any more learning, and Pop must have guessed that, because he closed the guidebook, drank his soda, then started making a little water dish out of his can. He used his pocket knife to cut off the bottom of it. Then he filled that with water from Momma's drinking glass and put it inside the new tank. He picked up the jar and slid the spider out. The tank already had airholes, but Pop made some of them bigger with his knife.

"There," he said. "Not a bad home for a spider."

Momma looked from me to Frita.

"Did you catch this spider for Gabe?" she asked. I knew Momma was thinking about me streaking by in my underwear. I held my breath, hoping she wouldn't tell Pop.

Frita nodded.

"I'm glad," Momma said. "He'll be a good pet. Fun to watch." She tapped on the glass tank. "What's his name?"

Funny how everyone thought a spider should have a name. Fortunately, I'd given this some thought.

"His name's Jimmy," I said, and Pop smiled.

"That's a good name," he said. "A darn good name."

## Chapter 11

# SIGNS AND PORTENTS

THAT NIGHT, AFTER FRITA WENT HOME, MOMMA, POP, ME, AND JIMMY the spider sat outside on the front steps. Momma said it was too hot to go inside. Felt cooler outdoors where a breeze might kick up every now and then. She leaned her head on Pop's shoulder and he kissed her neck instead of her cheek, which made her smile. Then we sat quiet while the neighbor's lights blinked off and the stars blinked on, one by one.

All around the trailer it got dark, but the fireflies lit up the night with hundreds of little lights. When one came close, Momma reached out and cupped it in her hand so I could watch it light up. She let it go by throwing it up in the air, only it stayed stuck to her palm like it wanted to stay there for good. Then Pop reached over and pushed it off with his thick, rough finger, but he was real gentle.

We sat outside until late. I didn't want to go to bed—ever. Felt right to sit out there with Momma and Pop, but once the moon was high, Pop nudged me indoors. I lay in my room on top of my bedsheets, listening to the crickets sing, and thought for sure I'd never fall asleep.

But I did.

I know, because I remember waking up.

It was almost three o'clock in the morning and I was having a nightmare. It was about spiders, but it wasn't about Jimmy. These spiders were people spiders and they were hanging on their webs, looking down on me and Frita.

In the dream, I'd lost Momma and Pop, and Frita was helping me look for them. We were walking through the swamp, hollering, only no one answered, so we walked faster and faster, trying to find them. My hands were clammy and my heart was pounding, and with every step my feet sunk deeper into the swamp muck.

"Momma?" I yelled. "Pop?"

It was dark in the swamp. Me and Frita tried to run, but we could hardly see and there were so many webs, we had to push them out of the way with our hands. We were in a sea of spiderwebs and they were full of all sorts of things—car fenders and corpses of kids half eaten by alligators. It was cold and smelled like muck, and I could feel a thousand eyes watching me.

Then I looked up and there *were* a thousand eyes watching me.

Spider eyes.

Hanging right above my head was a spider that looked

just like Duke Evans. He'd grown fangs where his missing teeth had been, and he was ready to pounce.

"Let's get out of here," I yelled.

I took off running, only I didn't get very far before I realized Frita wasn't with me. I stopped and turned around, and that's when I saw her. She was standing right under Duke's web, only this time it wasn't Duke who was up there, it was his daddy.

"Frita, run!" I yelled, but it was too late. The Mr. Evans spider reached out his huge spider claws and . . .

I sat bolt upright in bed, sweat dripping down my forehead. It had to have been a hundred degrees in my room, but I pulled the sheet up to my chin anyway. My eyes darted around, looking for spiderwebs. All I wanted to do was crawl into bed with Momma and Pop. Plus, I had to go to the bathroom something fierce, but I was sure the minute I put my feet down I'd feel the tickle of webs wrapping around my ankles. I stayed put until the sun came out and I heard Pop waking up. Then I sprinted to the bathroom.

Peeing never felt so good.

I knew right away I had to tell Frita about my dream. According to Frita, dreams were important. Her daddy read stories from the Bible where God warned people about stuff in their dreams. Mr. Wilson said those dreams were signs and portents—they told you what was going to happen in the future. If my dream was a portent, I wanted to tell Frita about it soon as I could, but I had to wait on account of it being Sunday and we had church.

"Stop fidgeting," Momma whispered during the service. I swung my legs and kicked at the pew in front of us.

"*Sit still,*" Pop said, giving me the evil eye.

I crossed my arms and scowled. I sure wished we could have gone to Frita's church, but Frita went to church in Rockford and I went to church in Hollowell. The only difference I could figure was that Frita's church was fun. I'd gone a couple times for special occasions, and when Mr. Wilson got going, he'd turn his sermon into a song. There was a huge choir that swayed and shouted behind the pulpit, and people yelled, "Amen" and "Preach it, brother" even though Mr. Wilson was not their brother.

This morning I'd said, "Couldn't we all go to Frita's church just this once?" But Momma said that church was for black people. Why we didn't just do some integrating I do not know, but we never did.

The only good thing about my church was that it let out a full hour before Frita's. That meant if I got on my bike the minute I'd changed out of my dress clothes, I could pedal over to Frita's house and be there by the time her family got back to cook Sunday dinner.

I pedaled extra fast and made the ride in only eight minutes, so I waited on Frita's front lawn. When the Wilsons pulled up in their station wagon, there I was. Frita waved from the window, but Terrance glared as he climbed out of the driver's seat. He looked like he might be headed down to the basement to punch things.

"What are you lookin' at?" he growled when he walked by. He had on a T-shirt that said BLACK POWER. I was pretty sure Mrs. Wilson didn't allow T-shirts at church on Sunday, and she frowned as Terrance stomped past. Terrance and Mrs. Wilson were always arguing about one thing or another. Mostly they argued about college. Mrs. Wilson said Terrance needed to think about the future—and that meant going to college. But Terrance said colleges were racist. He said they didn't want black people, so why should he go where he wasn't wanted? Terrance said *his* plan was to move to Atlanta and stay with his uncle Rory, who used to be in a group called the Black Panthers.

I watched as Terrance disappeared into the house. The front door slammed shut real hard, but Mrs. Wilson just shook her head. Then she turned to me.

"Hello, Gabe," she said at last. "You're here bright and early today." She took off her floppy hat. "Do you want some Sunday dinner?"

Mrs. Wilson always asked if I wanted Sunday dinner like it was a brand-new idea and she'd just thought of it. She knew what the answer was going to be because every time she asked me, I said yes.

"Yes, ma'am," I said, remembering my manners. Frita got out of the car and did a cartwheel on the lawn, then she somersaulted over to me. Mrs. Wilson sighed.

"You kids can play outside until dinner's ready, but Frita, you change your clothes before . . ."

It was too late. Me and Frita were halfway across the yard, headed for the pecan tree out back. Frita had on a dress with a wide ribbon and a bow in the back, plus she had on her dress shoes with new white socks, but she still beat me up the tree. I sat down two branches below her and tried to crack open a pecan.

"Two bucks says you can't guess what I dreamed about last night," I said.

Frita thought it over. "Spiders?"

I just about choked. "How'd you know that?" I asked.

Frita shrugged.

"Yeah," I said, "but you'll never guess what happened."

"What?"

"Let me tell you, it was the scariest dream I ever had in my whole life."

"Really?"

I crossed my heart and spit on the ground.

"Yup," I said. "I was awake all night because of it, and even after I woke up, I could still feel it."

Frita leaned over the branch. "What happened?"

Now I had her attention, so I told her about losing my

parents and walking through the spiderwebs, trying to find them.

". . . when I saw the spider that looked like Duke, I ran like heck, but you stayed put. You wouldn't go anywhere. Then I looked back over my shoulder and there was a spider waiting to get you, only it wasn't Duke. . . ." I made Frita lean in even closer. "It was his daddy!"

"No!"

"Uh-huh," I said. "He was reaching for you with his claws. I was so scared, I almost wet the bed."

Frita's eyes went wide like full moons. "He got me?" she whispered. I nodded and Frita said it again, only this time I could tell she was thinking hard.

"You think it means something?" she asked. "Think it's a sign?"

"Yup," I said. "I'm almost completely sure." I was growing more sure by the minute.

Frita took a deep breath. "Gabe," she said, "this is serious business. We're going to have to double our liberating. That must be what your dream meant—it was a warning so we wouldn't forget to make me brave too."

"What have you got to be scared—"

*"Frita! Gabe! Come wash up for dinner."*

Mrs. Wilson hollered out the back door and I jumped a mile. Frita swung off her branch, but I nearly fell out of mine. I landed with a thud.

"Frita, wait!" I said. "What are we going to do?"

She thought it over.

"I better make a list," she said. "Like you. Then we'll cross my stuff off too."

I swallowed hard. I'd never thought about Frita needing to be brave. I wondered what would be on her list.

"Come on," Frita said. "We can do it soon as dinner's over."

She took off, but I stood still, watching her go. The wind kicked up and carried with it a whiff of Mrs. Wilson's corn bread stuffing. Mrs. Wilson made the best corn bread stuffing in all of Georgia, but right then I didn't feel like eating. I had a churning feeling in the pit of my stomach that said there was going to be trouble.

Sure hoped it wasn't a sign or a portent.

# Chapter 12

# A BRUSSELS SPROUT SUNDAE

IF IT WAS UP TO ME, WE MIGHT HAVE FORGOTTEN ALL ABOUT THAT LIST and gone out to play after dinner, but when Frita makes up her mind, it's best not to stand in her way. Soon as the food was cleared off the table and her momma and daddy had gone outside to sit on the back porch and read the newspaper, Frita started making her list. Didn't take very long. I could tell she was taking it real serious, but she wouldn't let me see it.

"How many things you got?" I asked when she folded up her paper.

"Ten," she said.

*Only ten?!*

"But I'm not so sure I'm scared of all of them."

Not so sure? How could you not be sure? I had thirty-eight things on my list and I was scared of every single one of them. No doubts about it.

"What aren't you sure about?" I asked.

Frita shrugged. "Ummm . . . brussels sprouts."

"Brussels sprouts?" I said. "Those aren't scary."

Frita shook her head. "Are too," she said. "I might choke to death because they taste so bad."

I wondered if she was putting me on. Maybe she was making stuff up just to fill up her list.

"Your momma made brussels sprouts for dinner just the other night and nothing happened," I said, in case Frita had forgotten, but she just shrugged.

"That's true," she said, "but I didn't eat them. When you're not around to eat them for me, I hide them under other stuff, and if Momma notices, I pretend to cry and she gives me some other vegetable."

We were in Frita's living room and she was upside down again, only this time she was hanging off the couch. I narrowed my eyes.

"You're really scared of them?" I said. "For *real*?"

Frita nodded.

"Yup," she said. "Ever since I was a little kid. I even had a bad dream about eating brussels sprouts once. Must have been a sign and a portent."

I thought it over.

"Well, all right. Guess it's as good as anything."

We got up and went into the kitchen. There were leftover sprouts in the refrigerator, so I took them out and set them on the table.

"Want me to heat them up?" I asked.

Frita shook her head.

"I can't eat all of them," she told me. "How about just one?"

I wasn't sure that would do it. A person could eat one of anything. Even worms. I knew that for certain because Frankie Carmen made me eat a worm on the playground once and I'd swallowed it real quick. Hardly tasted a thing.

"How about three?" I said. Frita frowned, but she nodded.

I put three brussels sprouts into a bowl and handed her a spoon. She stared. Then she sniffed.

"You think a person can die from choking on some miserable food?" she asked. "Terrance said he read about a man who died eating cabbage. Hated it so much, he couldn't swallow, so the cabbage got stuck in his throat. Think that's true?"

Sounded possible to me. I thought about liver and how every time Momma made me eat it, I had to chew forever.

"Maybe you shouldn't risk it," I said, getting nervous, but Frita stuck out her chin.

"Nope," she said, "I'm doing it."

Frita put a brussels sprout in her mouth and chewed once, then she spat it out on the table and stuck out her tongue.

"I almost choked," she said. "I could feel it."

"Maybe that's what you're really afraid of," I said. "Choking . . ."

Frita nodded and we stared at the slimy sprout. I sure didn't want Frita to choke to death.

"You wouldn't choke if they didn't taste so bad," I suggested, "and they wouldn't taste so bad with something on them. How about ketchup?"

Frita wrinkled her nose.

"Relish?"

"No."

"Cheese?"

"Uh-uh."

"Mustard?"

"Nope."

"Chocolate sauce?"

Frita paused. "Maybe," she said, "if there was a lot of it and some ice cream, too."

I opened the freezer. There was a whole tub of vanilla ice cream, so I pulled it down and scooped some into Frita's bowl. Then I got out the chocolate sauce and mixed it all together so the brussels sprouts were completely covered.

"Better add some whipped cream," Frita said, so I got that out too, and piled some on top. Frita stared at her bowl, then she took a bite from the edge where there was only ice cream.

"Think we ought to cut the brussels sprouts into smaller pieces?" she asked. "That way, there's less to choke on." I shrugged. Didn't seem like it would make much difference, but I took out a knife and fork and cut each brussels sprout into little pieces. Then I licked all the ice cream off the knife.

"Better hurry before it melts."

Frita loaded up her spoon. "Gabe," she told me, real solemn, "if I choke to death, you can have my smiley face picture frame with our class picture in it."

"Okay," I said.

Then Frita closed her eyes and lifted the spoon to her mouth. I knew she had a big chunk of brussels sprout on there because I could see it through the ice cream. *Poor Frita,* I thought. I sure was glad I hadn't written down brussels sprouts. Frita stuck the spoon in her mouth and chewed. I waited for her to spit that mess out, but it didn't happen. Frita opened one eye. She swallowed without choking once.

"It's not so bad," she said. "Put some more chocolate sauce on there."

I poured it on so thick it was like chocolate soup, and Frita ate three more bites.

"Hey," she said at last, "I think I like this stuff."

My eyebrows shot up. "Really?"

"Yup," Frita said. She handed me the spoon and I loaded it up. "You've got to get plenty of chocolate sauce," she warned. "That way, you hardly taste the brussels sprouts."

Sure enough, Frita was right.

That's when Mrs. Wilson came into the kitchen. She stared at all the stuff I'd put on the counter and shook her head.

"I don't want to know," Mrs. Wilson said. "I just don't want to know."

That's exactly what Momma said about me streaking by in my underwear.

I looked at Frita and her eyes were twinkling something fierce.

"Gabe," she whispered, "it's working. *It's really working.*"

I knew she was talking about her plan, and even though I didn't want to admit it, for the first time I wondered if maybe she was right. Maybe we *would* overcome all our fears in time for the fifth grade.

*Chapter 13*

# A BUG'S BEST FRIEND

ONCE FRITA SUSPECTS SHE'S RIGHT, THERE'S NO STOPPING UNTIL she's positively certain.

"Let's cross something off our lists every week," Frita said, "only you'll have to cross off two or three because you've got so many."

That hardly sounded fair to me, but Frita put her hands on her hips.

"This is serious business," she reminded me. "Our entire future depends on it, so we can't be wasting any time."

"It's only the first of June," I said. But there was no arguing with Frita.

Straightaway we had to roller-skate on the yellow line in the middle of the highway because we'd seen that on TV once, so it was on both our lists. I might have picked something that *couldn't* have gotten us killed, but Frita assured me it would make us plenty brave. She was probably right too, only we never got to find out because Mrs. Wilson drove by just as we were getting started.

If there were three things Frita was never to do, they were playing on the highway, going near the Evans trailer, and lighting matches. Any one of those things threw Mrs. Wilson into a fit and let me tell you, *that* was something to be scared of. She pulled her car over and lifted us both up by the ears. Then we got a solid chewing out all the way home. It was worse than Momma on Moving-Up Day.

After that we were grounded, so I thought we might take a break from fear-busting, but Frita said we'd just have to find things to do at her house or my trailer since we couldn't go anywhere else. That was okay because I had plenty to choose from. First, we made a plan for what I'd do if I missed the school bus after school. Then I worked Momma's new blender even though it was huge and loud and I was certain I'd get my hand chopped off. After that, we practiced picking up earwigs, only I got pinched. But that turned out okay because the pinch didn't hurt hardly as bad as I thought it would, and Frita said that was just how she'd planned it.

When we were done being grounded, we roller-skated down the center of Frita's road. She said that was okay because it was our best try and best tries counted. And when it came to the lists, Frita was the judge.

"Long as we try our hardest, we can cross it off because once you've tried something, it's not so scary to try it again," she said.

That sort of made sense, but personally, I found I could be just as scared nineteen, maybe twenty times in a row. Took me eighteen tries to face down a loose cow in the cotton field. I kept taking off every time she snorted. By my eighteenth try she didn't pay me any mind at all. Just flicked her ear when I walked near her.

There was only one thing I utterly failed at, and it almost put an end to everything.

It was the middle of June and we were at Frita's house, reading through our lists. We were still keeping them secret because Frita said it would be more fun that way. I wasn't sure how exactly that made things fun, but I took Frita's word for it.

"It's your turn to pick," Frita said that afternoon, putting her list away in the special box under her bed.

"Nuh-uh," I said. "I just did one."

Frita gave me that look.

"You know you've got three times as many as I do," she reminded me. "I bet you still got half your list left."

I looked down and sure enough, Frita was right. I had *more* than half left. Drat.

"What're you gonna pick?" she asked.

I read through the things I hadn't crossed off. *Fifth grade, Duke Evans, alligators, the Evans trailer, Frita's basement, centipedes . . .*

Centipedes sure were gross, but I'd already tackled earwigs and spiders, so according to Frita's plan, I ought to be getting braver. I thought about Jimmy and how he really wasn't such a bad pet once I'd gotten used to him.

"Fine," I said. "How about centipedes?"

Frita grinned. "All right! I know just where to find one."

She grabbed my hand and pulled me down the hall.

"Our basement is full of them," Frita said. I stopped following, but Frita tightened her grip on my hand.

"Don't . . . be . . . a . . . scaredy-cat . . . ," Frita said, dragging me across the floor. "It's just a plain old basement and a little bug."

But Frita was wrong. There was nothing little about centipedes, and there was nothing plain about Frita's basement.

"What if Terrance is down there?"

Frita opened the basement door. The light was on and I could hear grunting noises and the *smack, smack* sound of someone pounding something.

"See?" I said. "He *is* down there. Guess we'll have to come back."

Frita pulled me down the first step. "Terrance won't care as long as we tell him we're coming," she said. She hollered down the steps, "ME AND GABE ARE COMING DOWN TO LOOK FOR CENTIPEDES!"

I waited for the rush of feet as Terrance ran up the steps to chase us away, but it didn't come. He was toweling off the sweat when we got to the bottom of the steps.

"Fine," he said. "I was done anyway." But he didn't say it nice. He glared at me. Then he yelled at Frita. *"Don't touch anything!"*

He snapped his towel at her, and she stuck out her tongue. Terrance took the stairs two at a time, and I watched him go, wondering if I'd ever be that big. I wondered what it felt like to have such long legs. Never getting any taller was number twenty-nine on my list, but there sure wasn't anything I could do about that.

Frita stood in the middle of the basement and looked around. The light was on this time because Terrance had been down there. The punching bags and panther drawings didn't look quite so big and scary when it wasn't dark.

"Look," said Frita, "it's not so bad."

She took a box off the shelf and put it on the floor. It was full of ornaments and a string of garland. "This is all our Christmas stuff. And here's that plastic pumpkin I used to take trick-or-treating."

She pulled down another box. "This one has all my baby clothes in it, and look, here's the doll Great-aunt Alma gave me." Frita wrinkled her nose. She hated dolls almost as much as she hated Great-aunt Alma.

I picked up the plastic pumpkin. This stuff *was* kind of neat. I had a pumpkin just like this one, only we didn't have a basement in the trailer, so mine was stashed in Momma and Pop's closet.

"What's in that one?" I asked, pointing to another box on the shelf along the wall. Frita got up on a stool and pulled down the boxes, one by one. It was almost like Christmas.

Until we found the centipede.

Frita might have forgotten all about centipedes if one hadn't crawled out of a box right when she was reaching in to take out a camping lantern. I was sitting on the floor, playing with Frita's old Matchbox cars, when out scampered a million legs and a slimy body. I jumped up and knocked over the box.

"All right!" Frita said, getting up to follow the centipede over to the wall. I hoped he'd be too fast to catch, but he stopped right by the furnace almost as if he was waiting for her to scoop him up.

"Frita," I said, "I changed my mind. I don't need to cross centipedes off my list because I already crossed off spiders and earwigs and I shoulda just written down bugs because that's what I meant. So, really, I'm done with—"

"Hush up," Frita said. She was crouching down, positioning her hands around the centipede. I looked away. Next time I peeked, she had her hands cupped real tight.

"Don't be scared," she told me. "Centipedes are soft and friendly. Let's name him so you'll feel like he's a pet. Or wait! Maybe I'll keep him. That way you'll have Jimmy and I'll have . . ." Frita thought it over. "Gilligan." Frita watched *Gilligan's Island* reruns on TV every week. "That's the perfect name!"

She was getting some excited, but I stared hard at her cupped hands. My eyes were huge as saucers.

"Daddy says fear is mind over matter," Frita told me. "If you don't mind it won't matter. Now, put out your hands."

I squeezed my eyes tight and tried to picture Jimmy in his tank. If he wasn't so bad, the centipede couldn't be much worse. I reached out my hands . . .

Frita plopped that centipede right into my palm and I

tried to cup him in there nice and tight, like Frita had, but I was too slow and he was too quick. He was up my arm in a flash.

"GET HIM OFF!" I hollered. I flicked my arm and the centipede fell onto the floor. Then before I even thought about it, I stomped him real good. I was dancing around in a circle, stomping that bug into one big centipede mash.

Only then I caught a glimpse of Frita. Her eyes were huge and both her hands were over her mouth.

"You're killing Gilligan," she choked at last. I couldn't tell if she was going to cry or pound me.

That's when I stopped stomping.

I looked down at the splotch on the basement floor and all sorts of guilt flooded in. Frita knelt down to look and her bottom lip quivered. She gave me the worst look I'd ever seen.

"You killed my pet," she said. "He wasn't even hurting you. He was just crawling around, that's all." Then she sniffed hard. "Gabriel King," she said, "you're not getting any braver at all!"

Frita turned and marched up the stairs. I heard the front door slam and I knew she'd gone out back to sit in the pecan tree. That's when my stomach started to churn. I thought about the way Frita's eyes had gotten big and round like mine did when I was the most scared. Maybe dead things were on Frita's list.

Then *my* eyes got big and round because I'd killed Frita's pet just because I was chicken. Maybe she'd never forgive me.

Frita being mad at me was number twenty-three.

There was only one thing to do. I took a little plastic cup out of one of the boxes and even though it was gross, I scooped that squished-up bug into the cup. We'd have a real decent burial for Gilligan. Then I'd promise never to kill another bug again. If that's what it took to get Frita to forgive me, I'd be Gabriel King, a bug's best friend.

# Chapter 14

# CORPSES AND DOBERMANS

Frita was real sore at me after that—despite the real nice funeral we held in her backyard. She didn't call me on the phone or ask me to come over for two whole days, and when we finally did get together, it was another day and a half before things were back to normal. Only they weren't *exactly* back to normal. Frita didn't mention our lists again once. Not even when I told her I'd crossed off number twenty-three since she'd forgiven me.

Life was strained. Summer was at its peak—you couldn't move an inch without breaking a sweat—and there's nothing worse than suffering in the heat while your best friend is sore at you. The only saving grace was the Bicentennial. It was on its way and we were real excited.

The last week of June, me and Frita met up in Hollowell to get ice cream cones. I'd saved up my allowance every day since I'd squished the centipede, so it was my treat. Frita got a strawberry cone and I got a vanilla one and we sat on the lawn in front of the town hall to eat them. That was a good spot because you could listen in on everyone's conversations.

"You got those fireworks set for the Fourth, Joe?"

"How about those sparklers for the kids?"

"Who's in charge of the parade floats this year?"

Everyone had something to say, and it was fun listening to them with ice cream dripping down your chin. At least, it was fun until Duke and his pop pulled up in their old monster truck. I'd been trying not to think about Duke all summer, but now I remembered him right quick.

"Let's go," I said to Frita, but she stayed put.

"They're not gonna chase *me* away," she said. She was pretending to be brave, but I noticed how she watched real careful while Mr. Evans climbed out of the truck. Duke climbed out after him and said something to his pop. Then he glared at me and Frita, but she glared straight back. Mr. Evans glanced over at us but he didn't say anything. He just kept walking to the general store.

"See?" said Frita. "That wasn't so bad." But I wondered who she was trying to convince—me or herself. I was glad Mr. Evans hadn't called Frita any names again, but I didn't want to stick around until they came back.

"C'mon," I said. "Let's go back to my house and make another obstacle course."

I tried to pull Frita up with me, but she didn't budge. Her eyes narrowed into slits like she was getting an idea. Then they started to sparkle again. I couldn't decide if that was a good thing or a bad thing. Only thing I knew for certain was it meant trouble.

"I got a better idea," Frita said.

"What?" I asked, real suspicious. I sure hoped it didn't involve bugs.

Frita's chin jutted out like it did when she got something in her head she was going to be stubborn about. "Gabe," she said, "it's time to do some liberatin'. "

The thing about trouble is, if you think you're going to land in it, you can be pretty certain you're right. One minute I was sitting outside the town hall with an ice cream cone, and the next minute I was crouched in a pricker bush outside Duke Evans's trailer.

Looked like our fear-busting was back in business.

"You sure we should do this?" I asked, peering between the branches.

"Yup," said Frita. "Duke's trailer is on your list, right? Well, it's on mine too, so now's our chance."

We were just a few feet away from the edge of Duke's yard.

"What if someone's home?"

"We know they're not," Frita said, "that's why we've got to do it now."

I sniffed the air, remembering what Duane Patterson said about Mrs. Evans's corpse. I didn't smell anything, but there wasn't any wind today.

"Duane said they've got Dobermans in there," I whispered.

Frita wiped her brow.

"I don't hear any barking," she said, but we both stayed

real silent just in case. I hadn't put Dobermans on my list, but that was only 'cause I hadn't thought of them at the time. Truth was, I'd rank them right close to spiders.

"Didn't your momma and daddy say not to come around here?" I said.

I could hear Mrs. Wilson's voice in my head. *"Don't you go near that place. You hear me, Frita Wilson?"* She'd said it a hundred times. Then I thought about what Pop had said about me and Frita needing to watch ourselves. Maybe this was what he'd meant.

"Pop said we ought to be careful—" I started, but Frita interrupted me.

"Hush up," she said. "Didn't I tell you that liberatin' is serious business?"

I nodded.

"Well, there's no kind of serious business that isn't risky. Besides, we're watching out, aren't we? Why else do you think we're in the bushes?"

I had to admit Frita had a point.

"Come on," she said. "Let's check things out. I bet you two dollars it's not so scary once we get up close."

Frita darted out of the bushes, but I grabbed her back again and held on tight.

"Don't be a scaredy-cat," Frita told me, real stern. "It's broad daylight."

Frita pulled loose of my grip. She dodged an old tire and a car fender, then she hesitated. We'd never been this close before. I closed my eyes and held my breath. Then I opened one eye and watched as Frita darted the rest of the way to the door. She touched it with her palm, then looked back over her shoulder and grinned.

"See?" she said. "Not so scary. I told you."

Far as I was concerned, Frita could have all the glory. I stayed planted in my spot, but Frita didn't put up with that.

"Get over here, Gabriel King," she hollered. "You can't cross this off your list unless you get out of that pricker bush."

I crawled out and scooted around to the back of the trailer where Frita was trying to see in the back window. There were a thousand voices screaming inside my head and every one of them was telling me to run, but Frita couldn't hear them.

"Let's see if Mrs. Evans's corpse is really in there," she said. "I'll give you a boost."

I shook my head. "No way."

"You have to," Frita told me. "I'm too big for you to boost up, and we can't see in even on tiptoes. All you got to do is look."

"What if I see her?"

Frita was making her hands into a cup shape so I could step into them.

"Well, then you can cross corpses off your list too."

Huh. I hadn't thought of that. I guessed the quickest way out of there was to take a peek, so I put one foot in Frita's palms and rested the other one on the side of the trailer to balance. Then I put my hands on the window and pulled myself up. The old wood was scratchy beneath my palms.

"What do you see?" Frita asked. "Do you see Mrs. Evans? Is she dead?"

Frita was pouring out questions, but truth was I couldn't be sure exactly what I saw. The old curtain hanging over the window made everything look ghostly white.

"I see some furniture," I said, "and there's a pile of clothes in one corner. There're some shoes in the pile and . . ." Wait! Were those shoes, or were they feet? Sure did look like feet. Maybe underneath that pile of rags was Duke's dead momma. Maybe that's why our parents didn't want us near here. I turned to look at Frita, but all I saw was Mrs. Evans coming at me with a broom.

*"You kids get away from here!"*

Frita let loose such a high-pitched scream, a dog started yelping from across the street. She pulled her hands out from under my feet so fast, I didn't know what had happened. One minute I was peeking in the window trying to trace the outline of a corpse, and the next minute I was lying on my back in a cloud of dust and Mrs. Evans was raising her broom high above my head.

For a minute I was frozen stiff, but then that broom was coming down quick. I rolled onto my side and clambered to my feet. I felt like I'd been hit by an eighteen-wheeler, but I got up and ran like the dickens.

*"Don't you kids be coming around here! I don't want to catch you near this place ever again. If I do, I'll . . ."*

I could hear her yelling after us halfway back to my place. On every other occasion Frita could run way faster than me, but I was so scared I clear out beat her to my trailer. I got there a full minute before she did.

Frita could barely catch her breath.

"What did you . . . Can you believe . . . Did you see . . ."

She lay down on the ground, sprawled out like a limp rag doll, and I sat down beside her, my heart still thumping.

"Gabe," she said at last, breathing hard, "I think we nearly got ourselves killed."

That was the God's honest truth. We'd gone in worrying about one corpse and come out worrying about two.

# Chapter 15

# OFF A HIGH BRANCH

ONE THING I LEARNED ABOUT LIBERATING: SOMETIMES IT'S NOT SO easy to decide when it's done. Now we were twice as scared of the Evans trailer as we'd been before, but Frita said that had most definitely been our best try, so we crossed it off in black Magic Marker. Then we decided to take a breather.

July first, Frita came over and brought an article from *Life* magazine. It was all about the Bicentennial, so we propped it up against Jimmy's spider tank so we could both see it at the same time. We lay in the grass on our stomachs, reading it, and every now and then we'd turn the magazine around so Jimmy could see the pictures.

We were looking at a two-page spread of fireworks when Frita asked her question.

"Think we should go to the fireworks in Hollowell?" she asked, studying the page.

"Where else would we go?"

"We could go to the ones in Rockford."

"Why would we do that?" I asked.

Frita shrugged.

We were quiet for a minute, but then she said, "Terrance told me there wouldn't be any black people at the ones in Hollowell. He said they'd all be going to Rockford."

I wondered why it made a difference. Never seemed to bother Frita before.

"Terrance said white people aren't celebrating *our* independence. He says they're only celebrating the independence of white people."

Huh. I thought we were celebrating everyone's independence.

"Momma and Pop and me are celebrating your independence," I said, "and we're going to Hollowell."

Frita shrugged like it was no big deal.

"I was just wondering," she said. Then she flipped the page around so Jimmy could see. "You think Mr. Evans will be there?"

She said it real casual, but I could tell she'd been gearing up to ask me that. I hadn't thought about it none, but I supposed he would be. "Yup," I said.

Frita flipped off her sandals and wiped the sweat from her brow.

"No big deal," she said, tapping on Jimmy's tank. Then she turned over on her back and changed the subject. "Want to go swimming in the catfish pond?"

Frita was already wearing her bathing suit top with shorts because it was too hot to wear other clothes. Swimming sounded real good, except there was always a clump of sixth-graders at the catfish pond, and two of them were sure to be Duke and Frankie.

"We could use the sprinkler," I said.

"Sprinklers are for babies." Frita looked at me like she knew exactly what I was thinking. "It's time we did more liberatin' anyway."

Frita stood up. "I'll do something off my list if you come swimming."

Now my ears perked up because I was always interested in what was on Frita's list, and it *was* pretty hot out.

"What's left on your list?" I asked.

"The rope swing . . . mostly."

"Mostly?"

Frita nodded.

"It's on my list too," I said, but that was the wrong thing to say, because Frita got all excited.

"Go ask your momma if we can go," she said, standing up. Then she picked up Jimmy's tank and twirled him like a ballerina.

"This will make us brave for sure," she said.

Maybe Frita was going to be brave, but I knew I was headed to almost certain death. I said I'd do five other things off my list if we stayed home and used the sprinkler, but Frita was being a locomotive again.

"Just wait," she told me. "After this you'll feel so brave, you'll be first in line for the fifth grade."

Fat chance of that. Besides, the sixth-graders never let anyone else use the rope swing. It was an unwritten rule. But apparently Frita didn't intend on following it.

"No one's going to tell me what I can or can't do," Frita said as we walked to the catfish pond. "We'll just march right up to that tree and climb to the top before anyone can stop us. It's only fair. Ain't their tree to . . ."

Frita stopped mid-sentence. We'd reached the pond, and there in a clump, just like I'd suspected, was a whole group of sixth-graders. Smack in the middle of them were Duke Evans and Frankie Carmen.

Soon as I saw them, my whole body tightened up like a dishcloth that was being wrung tight. Duke and Frankie were real close to us, standing on the opposite side of the cypress tree, chewing on candy cigarettes and talking to some girls. Any minute now they'd turn around and see us.

"Let's go home," I whispered, but Frita shook her head.

"No way," she said. "We got just as much right to be here as them, and I want to go swimming. They're not going to scare me." She started forward, but I pulled her back again.

"What if Duke wants to fight? You punched him in the nose, remember?"

Frita made a face. "I can whup Duke Evans and Frankie Carmen both," she said, "and they know it. Now, come on."

Frita was right about one thing. She *could* whup Duke and Frankie both and they probably wouldn't risk getting walloped in front of girls, but I bet they could think up something else to do. I stared at them, then up at the rope swing hanging off the high branch. I was so nervous, I could feel the waterworks gearing up, but I choked them down and Frita grabbed my hand.

"You can do it," she whispered. The look in her eyes said she believed it even if I didn't.

"You sure?" I asked.

"I'm sure," she told me.

I swallowed hard and let her pull me toward the tree.

My heart was pounding fast and my throat felt full, like I couldn't breathe, but Frita held tight and neither Duke nor Frankie turned around to notice us. Frita slipped off her sandals and shorts, real silent, and I took off my T-shirt and sneakers extra fast and left them next to Frita's stuff. Then we climbed up the tree, quick and quiet as we could.

The bark was rough against my toes, but it was easy to get my footing. I kept looking down at the ground below, and the higher we climbed, the more certain I was that there was no way I'd survive. But I couldn't turn around now. Frita and I sat down on the tree limb facing each other, gathering our courage. For a minute we were completely silent. I watched her face and listened to the sound of my heartbeat. *Thump, thump, thump, thump.*

Then they saw us.

"Hey, look!"

Duke was pointing up, and my heart sunk. I looked at Frita, real panicky, but she kept her eyes locked on mine.

"You can do it," she said. "I got faith . . ."

Down below, the rest of the kids were laughing and pointing too.

"It's Gabe and Frita up in a tree."

"K-I-S-S-I-N-G . . ."

"Too scared to jump? You've got to stand up first, you know. "

They were right under us, laughing and whistling and calling out. I closed my eyes because this was *real* trouble.

"You stuck? Want us to call your mommies?"

"Better call Gabe's pop," I heard Duke say. "He always calls his pop. My Pop could take all three of them."

That's when Frita stood up. She scowled something fierce. "Gabe," she said, "I'm going."

For one minute I thought she meant she was going home—like maybe we'd climb down that tree and walk right past those hecklers—but I should have known better. Frita stood up and looked at me one last time, then she leaned out, grabbed that rope, and swung right off the tree branch.

Even though she was my best friend and I knew what she was going to do, for a minute she was like someone I'd never met. Someone incredible.

Frita landed with a huge splash, and that was just about

enough for me. I wanted to climb down right then, and I would have except for Duke.

"You'll never make it," he yelled.

I stood up and stared down at the water. Frita waved, and I felt like I was a hundred miles high. I was sure I would break my neck. The water below was brown and murky, and you couldn't tell how deep it was in the middle. Maybe hundreds of feet. I imagined letting go of that rope and plunging in. Once I splashed down, I'd turn and turn. What if I forgot which way was up and couldn't keep my breath?

"What's the matter, Shrimp?" Duke yelled. "Can't reach the rope?"

My mouth went dry. I hadn't even thought of that. I forced my eyes away from the water long enough to watch for the rope. It was still swinging from when Frita let go of it, and the next time it came toward me, I reached for it. I missed and my whole body leaned forward, back, forward, back . . . I waved my arms like a propeller and I heard laughter, but I got my balance. I watched for the rope again and this time I leaned a little farther out.

I caught it just like one of those trapeze guys in the circus and held it tight. I closed my eyes and felt my feet leave the tree branch. After that, all I felt was my heart thump-thumping and the roughness of the rope burning my palms. Then I let go and I was turning and turning in the water. For a minute I didn't know which way was up, but then I *was* up, breathing in big gulps of sweet air.

I splashed like crazy, but when I stopped and looked back to shore, there were Duke and Frankie staring with their jaws on the ground.

I looked at Frita and she was grinning real huge.

"I knew it," Frita said. "I knew you could do it."

And she was right. I had done it. Me and Frita bobbed and grinned in the water, and back on shore Duke and Frankie waved our clothes and Frita's sandals in the air, then swung them into the trees.

"Hey," they yelled, "come and get 'em."

But we didn't care. They could take our shoes and shorts, but they couldn't take our courage.

# Chapter 16

# PERSEVERING THROUGH
# A FINE DINNER

THERE'S NOTHING LIKE SUCCESS TO BOOST YOUR CONFIDENCE. LEAST that's what Frita said after the rope swing. That made sense, only I wondered if confidence was the same thing as courage. We'd jumped off the rope swing five more times after the sixth-graders left, but I still didn't want to go to the fifth grade. But Frita didn't seem to notice that part. She was too excited.

"The way things are going," Frita said, "we'll be completely liberated by the Bicentennial."

We were sitting in her bedroom, drawing pictures and listening to her transistor radio. It was shaped like a plastic spaceship and we had to adjust the antenna to get any music to come in. I pushed it all the way over to the side like I was working at fixing it, but really I was thinking.

"You decide which fireworks you're going to?" I asked.

Frita gave me a look like she hardly knew what I was talking about. "Hollowell," she said. "Where else?"

I wondered when she'd made up her mind, but I didn't ask because that was the one I wanted her to pick.

"We gonna stay up all night in the tent afterward?" Frita asked.

I'd been waffling on that decision. Last year we'd tried to stay up all night, but I'd gotten scared on account of what had sounded like a black bear but had turned out to be a raccoon. After that I'd had to go inside and sleep with Momma.

"Maybe," I said, and Frita put both hands on her hips.

"Gabriel King," she said, "you got to get you some perseverance."

I wasn't so sure what perseverance was all about, so Frita tried to explain.

"It's pushing on," she said. "Toward the high mark."

That was part of a hymn we sang in church, and I wondered if Frita really knew what perseverance meant or if she was just making it up. Then I thought about all the things I needed and how there were so many of them. Courage, integrity, faith, confidence, perseverance . . . Sure would be easier to sit back with my feet up and maybe eat a snack.

Frita got up and put her drawing away.

"What have you got left on your list?" she said, pulling out the special shoe box from under the bed where we kept it. I took out my list and read over everything real careful. There were a bunch of fears we hadn't crossed off yet, but I wanted to pick the easiest one. Only this time Frita didn't wait. She plucked the list right out of my hands.

"Let me read it," she said, climbing onto her bed. "It's almost done anyway."

Then, before I could stop her, she started reading it out loud.

"Number one, fifth grade. Number two, Duke Evans. Number three, Frankie Carmen. Number four, spiders. Number five, alligators. Number six, Terrance . . ."

Frita stopped reading.

"Terrance?!"

I sure wished I hadn't written that one down.

"You're scared of Terrance?!"

"No," I said, even though I was lying.

"You wrote it down," she said. "Once you write something down, it's true."

"Is not."

"Is too."

"Not."

"Too."

"Not."

That's when Mrs. Wilson came in. "You kids getting along?" she asked.

I glared at Frita so she'd know she better not breathe a word of this to her momma. She paused and handed me back my list, but then she said, "Can Gabe stay for dinner?"

Mrs. Wilson nodded. She never said no when it came to feeding me because she had the idea Momma didn't feed me enough. And Mrs. Wilson did serve more food than Momma. When Momma served dinner, there were always three things. Sometimes, it was pork chops, green beans, and applesauce, or else it was mac-n-cheese, peas, and bread, but it was always three, and one of those was always a vegetable, so that meant there were only two that counted. When Mrs. Wilson made dinner, she made about ten things. There'd be some sort of meat, and then a couple vegetables so a body could choose what was most tolerable, and then there'd be corn bread, mashed potatoes, rice and beans . . . *Mmm, mmm*, Mrs. Wilson was a good cook.

"You can stay if your mother says it's okay," Mrs. Wilson said. "Why don't you go call her?"

I jumped off the bed, real excited, but then I stopped. It occurred to me there was probably a reason Frita was inviting me to dinner and it probably had to do with Terrance.

I had to weigh everything real careful.

"What are you making for dinner?" I asked. Mrs. Wilson was hanging up some of Frita's clothes in the closet, but she stopped and turned around, surprised. I'd never asked what she was making before.

"Corned beef, some collard greens, a bit of okra, corn bread, little bit of brown rice, applesauce . . . oh, and I've made bread pudding with sweet brandy sauce for dessert. That all right with you, Gabe?" She was smiling like something was kind of funny, but she didn't laugh.

I never could resist bread pudding.

"All right," I said at last.

Mrs. Wilson turned back around.

"Oh, good," she said.

"Is Terrance coming to dinner tonight?" Frita asked, real sweet.

Mrs. Wilson turned around again and put one hand on her hip. As Frita would say, it was common knowledge that everyone at the Wilson household came to dinner every night, no matter what.

"What are you two up to?" Mrs. Wilson asked, real suspicious.

"Nothing," Frita said. Then she grabbed my arm. "Come on, Gabe. Let's call your momma so we can go outside before dinner."

"What are you going to do?" I asked Frita when we were outside knocking moss off the trees with two big sticks. I was nervous, so I kept missing.

"Nothing," Frita said. "I'm just going to make sure you and Terrance get to talk. Momma always says things would be all right if black people and white people could just sit down and talk over a fine dinner."

I stopped swiping at the moss. *Huh.* I sure hadn't thought about me and Terrance as black people and white people. I'd thought about us as a big, pounding, scary person and a little wimpy person who doesn't want to get pounded. The way Frita put it made it seem like a big deal, and that couldn't be good.

By the time Mrs. Wilson called us in to dinner, I was wishing I'd said no, even if we were having bread pudding. Then, when we went inside to wash our hands, Terrance was already at the sink, only he wasn't standing right next to it, so when me and Frita ran in full blast, we took his spot. Terrance narrowed his eyes.

"Twerps," he growled. He stormed out of the bathroom. I gulped, and Frita looked over at me.

"He don't mean anything."

Maybe, I thought, or maybe *not*.

Frita went into the dining room and sat down next to her daddy, who was just taking off his tie and stretching his long legs under the table.

"Hello there, beautiful," he said to Frita. Then he turned to me. "Gabriel," he said, nodding as I pulled out my chair.

"*Helllooo,* Mrs. Wilson," he said when Mrs. Wilson brought out the corned beef. She leaned over to put the tray down and he kissed her cheek.

She smiled and said, "Hello, Mr. Wilson," like it was some inside joke between the two of them. Me and Frita reached for the corn bread and collard greens and started passing stuff around. We had everything all passed before Terrance even came to the table. Mrs. Wilson scowled because he was late, but she didn't say anything.

I took a deep breath before launching into my meal and it was a good thing I did, because I forgot about the prayer. When you ate dinner at the Wilsons', there was always a prayer and it was always a long one. Mr. Wilson started in slow at first, but then he'd get into it and his voice would start sounding like a song. Mrs. Wilson would say *mmm-hmm* while Mr. Wilson prayed, and the whole time we'd be holding hands round the table. I sure was glad I didn't have to hold Terrance's hand.

By the time the prayer was over, my mouth was watering something fierce. I took a huge bite of corned beef immediately after Mr. Wilson said "Amen." Frita scraped her collard greens into a pile under her corn bread so it would look like she'd eaten them.

"Terrance, Gabe wants to know what your favorite color is," Frita asked out of nowhere after we'd all been eating a bit. I nearly choked on my okra, and Terrance made a face.

"What business is it of his?"

Mr. Wilson scowled. "Terrance, tell the boy your favorite color," he said. "Won't hurt you to be civil." Mrs. Wilson was shaking her head like she was some fed up.

Terrance paused, sarcastic-like, then he said, "Black. What's yours? White?"

I paused too. "No," I said, "it's blue mostly, but sometimes green when I can't make up my mind."

Terrance laughed like I'd said something stupid, and Frita picked at her corned beef. We all went back to eating again, but not for long.

"Gabe wants to know what your hobbies are," Frita said, as if the last question hadn't been enough.

This time Terrance's face twisted up like squash vine.

"Why doesn't the twerp ask me himself?"

Mrs. Wilson glared. "Don't you speak about our guest that way," she said. I just sat there looking from Frita to Terrance to Mrs. Wilson. I was sinking lower and lower into my chair, and that was hard to do because the Wilsons' chairs were the wooden kind with the straight backs. Mostly I ended up hunched over the table. I kicked Frita underneath it.

"Ouch."

Mrs. Wilson gave the two of us the evil eye, and I knew I better hurry up and ask something quick before everyone got mad.

"Umm. Do you have your driver's license?" I asked. I already knew the answer, but it was the only thing I could think of.

Terrance sat back in his chair. He put one arm over the empty chair next to him and eyed me real cold. He'd hardly eaten a thing.

"You want to know what I do for fun?" he asked, ignoring the question about the driver's license. I nodded even though I was pretty sure I didn't want to know.

"I fight oppression," Terrance said. "You know what that is, Twerp?"

The funny thing was, this time Terrance didn't say it mean. He said it like maybe he really wanted to know if I knew what oppression was. I thought maybe I did.

"I know," I said, nodding. "Once I found a stray dog and Pop wouldn't let me keep him. I was real oppressed about it because I thought Pop might say yes."

Mrs. Wilson laughed into her napkin. She was trying not

to, but I could tell what she was doing. Mr. Wilson smiled too, but Terrance got real mad.

"What?" Terrance said. "What kind of a stupid answer is that?"

Mr. Wilson looked at Terrance like he was saying something serious with his eyes. Then he turned to me. "Gabe," he said, "it's not your fault you don't know what oppression is. White people don't always teach their kids about oppression, because they don't think they have to know about it. But that's not the case, is it? We all need to know what oppression is or else how will we fight it?"

I swallowed hard. "Yes, sir," I said, even though I still didn't know what I'd gotten wrong about it. Mr. Wilson set down his fork.

"Oppression is when you're put down," he said. "It's when you don't have the freedom to be who you want to be because someone else doesn't believe you should have that freedom. Oppression is one person keeping down another person because of the color of his skin, or the language he speaks, or the religion he practices."

Mr. Wilson was starting to sound like a preacher again. He was getting louder and taking up a rhythm, like he did when he was praying. It was like being at church only I was getting my own personal sermon.

I listened real careful and tried to think if I knew what Mr. Wilson was talking about. At first I thought I didn't, but then I remembered Pop's story about Jimmy Carter and the White

Citizens Council. Only this time I thought about it in a different way from how I'd thought about it the first time. This time, instead of thinking about what happened to Jimmy Carter, I thought about what it must have felt like for the black people in Plains who had a whole group forming against them. I bet they felt some oppressed, and they must have had to be real brave.

I told that to Mr. Wilson and he looked surprised.

"Gabe," he said, "that's exactly right." He looked at Terrance across the table, but Terrance only snorted like he didn't care what I'd said.

Mrs. Wilson cut me an extra piece of corn bread. "I think we've got ourselves another Peace Warrior," she said, winking at Mr. Wilson.

No one had ever called me that in my whole entire life. I wondered if a chicken could really become a warrior, but Frita grinned like it was already true.

"You can join our group," she told me, "just like me and Terrance."

I looked at Terrance, but he didn't look too excited about that idea. He got up from the table and took his plate into the kitchen.

"Can I be excused?" he asked, but he said it after he'd already gotten up, and then he left even though Mrs. Wilson didn't answer. She sighed.

"Don't mind him," she said, dishing everyone some more corned beef.

I stared down the hallway where Terrance had disappeared, but Mr. Wilson poked me in the stomach.

"A warrior's got to eat," he said with his mouth full, and it was okay because I suspected Mr. Wilson was a warrior too, and sometimes warriors have to talk with their mouths full.

## Chapter 17

# INSIGHT INTO A POUNDING

AFTER DINNER, WHEN WE WERE DOING THE DISHES, FRITA WANTED TO know if I was still scared of Terrance. She said it was important because being scared of people was the worst kind of scared, and if I was going to get to the fifth grade, we had better get this one right. I thought it over extra hard, then I told Frita I might still be the teeniest bit afraid.

"Well, how come?" she asked.

I shrugged. "I dunno. He's pretty grumpy all the time and I don't think he likes me any. Plus, he beats on you a lot. How come you're not scared of him?"

Frita gave me a funny look. "Scared of Terrance?" she asked. "He's not scary. He just beats up on me 'cause I like it, and he's grumpy all the time because he doesn't want to go to college, but most of the time he's okay."

I wondered if that was true, but Frita put down the last plate and studied me hard.

"We've got to fix this," she said. "You need yourself some insight."

I groaned. If insight meant looking in at something, I was pretty sure I could do without it. Didn't seem like I ought to get any closer to Terrance than I already was. But Frita latched onto my sleeve and pulled me down the hall.

When we got to Terrance's room, she pushed open the door and went straight in without knocking.

"What are you doing?" Terrance growled, like we'd barged in on something top secret. I turned around and started to back out, but Frita stayed put. She also kept her grip on my sleeve, so I was like one of those cartoon characters running in place.

"Gabe's afraid of you," she said, just like that. I turned about five shades of red and I could feel all that color creeping from my neck to the very tips of my ears.

Terrance laughed. "Good," he said.

That's when Frita started to cry, only it wasn't real crying, it was fake crying—I could tell—but Terrance didn't seem to know the difference. He was sitting at his desk, reading a book called *What Should I Do With My Life?* First he stopped reading, and then he glanced at me. I would have bolted if it hadn't been for Frita's tight grip.

"Quit that," he said to Frita, but he didn't say it mean. She sniffled.

"I won't," she said. "Gabe is my best friend and you're mean to him. He thinks you hate him." She threw herself onto Terrance's bed and muffled her face in his pillow. Terrance just sighed and picked Frita up by the ankles so she was hanging upside down.

"Come on, Frito," he said. "I don't hate Gabe. He's a twerp is all. Quit it."

Terrance was trying to sound tough like he usually does, but you could tell his heart wasn't in it. His voice was soft instead of rough. He swung Frita up in the air and dumped her on his bed. Frita stopped crying.

"Tell Gabe you like him."

Terrance made a face, but Frita looked at him with extrabig eyes and stuck one lip out. Terrance glared at her, then at me.

"You're okay, Twerp," he said.

"Tell him he can be a Peace Warrior, like us."

Terrance snorted. "He can try," he said, like he didn't believe it, but he didn't say it mean.

"Tell him he can sit on your bed," Frita said. Then she giggled, which gave everything away. I could tell Terrance was catching on. He looked at Frita, then back at me, and for a second I thought he was going to pound me for sure. He lunged right toward me just like he lunged toward his punching bags, but then he picked me up, flipped me over, and swung me on the bed, like he'd swung Frita.

"Fine," he said. "Go ahead. Sit on the bed if you want." Only this time he was *almost* laughing. All the color drained from my face, then filled back in again. I landed on the bed with a bounce. Maybe Frita was right. It was kind of fun getting tossed around like that.

Frita hopped off, but Terrance grabbed her round the waist and flung her up again.

"Come on, Frito. You said you wanted to sit on my bed. Go ahead. Put your stinky, dirty feet all over it."

Frita was giggling something fierce now and I slid off the bed purely on accident. Terrance grabbed me up like I weighed nothing and threw me in a heap on his pillow.

"You gotta stay there now. Frito says you want to sit on my bed, so you better sit on my bed."

Frita hopped off again and he flung her back on, and then we both hopped off and he caught one of us in each arm and flung us both.

"I'm twerp lifting," he said. "How much you weigh, Twerp? Eighty pounds? I bet I could bench-press eighty pounds."

Terrance picked me up and pretended like he was lifting a real heavy weight. Frita screamed and knocked him in the stomach with a pillow. Terrance said "Oof" and then he started to topple while he was still holding me in the air, and I screamed because I thought he was going to drop me for real, only he didn't and next thing you know, me and Frita were both pounding him with pillows.

That's when Mrs. Wilson came by and stood in the door. *"Mmm mmm mmm,"* she said, shaking her head, but she was smiling too, like everything might turn out okay after all.

# Chapter 18

# FIREWORKS

It was on account of Terrance that I came up with my idea about Mr. Evans. Me and Frita were on our way back from town the next afternoon when Frita brought him up. We were walking along the old dirt road through clouds of hot, dry dust, and I could barely see Frita through the haze, but she was talking real steady, so it didn't matter.

"You think Mr. Evans is mean as he seems?" she asked. "Because I saw him in town the other day and he was talking to Mr. Al and he didn't seem so bad, but I don't know. . . ."

Usually I let Frita ramble on, but I was feeling pretty good about me and Terrance, so I started thinking.

"You're pretty scared of him. He's on your list, isn't he?" I said.

If I wasn't Frita's best friend, she might have socked me in the jaw. A body didn't accuse Frita Wilson of being scared without a dang good reason.

"You're scared of him too," Frita pointed out. "And besides, my daddy *told* me to be scared of him. I'm *supposed* to be."

"Thought you said this was serious business," I said,

"and that serious business meant we couldn't always listen to our pops."

Frita frowned, but I kept right on going.

"Maybe you should try and talk to him like I talked to Terrance. See how great that turned out?"

"That's not the same thing," Frita said, but she didn't look so sure.

"How come?"

"Because Terrance is my brother, and Mr. Evans is . . ."

"Well, he's an adult, ain't he? How bad can he be?"

Frita didn't say anything. I knew she was thinking about him calling her that name on Moving-Up Day. I'd thought of that too, a whole bunch of times, and I sure wished he could take it back. Maybe Mr. Evans wished the same thing.

"Maybe he's sorry for calling you that name," I said. "He was probably just mad about you and Duke fighting, like you were mad at me for killing Gilligan. That's what you could talk to him about. You could tell him you're sorry, and that you were just sticking up for me, and then you could ask if he'd talk to Duke so he wouldn't be so mean next year. I bet he'd do it too, because that's what pops do."

Suddenly I felt like a real Peace Warrior. I was going to make peace between Frita, Mr. Evans, me, and Duke all at once and then we really would cross everything off our lists by the Bicentennial.

But this time it was Frita who didn't look so sure.

"When would I talk to him?" she asked. "I can't just knock on the trailer door or else Duke and Mrs. Evans will be there."

This was a good point, but my plan was growing bigger in my mind.

"You can talk to him at the fireworks. He'll be there for certain. It'll be the perfect time because there will be all sorts of other people around, so if he's mean, he can't do anything. But if he's not, you'll find out and you can cross him off your list. Then we'll be completely brave, just like you said."

"I guess it's an okay plan," Frita said.

"It's the best plan ever," I told her. "Just wait and see."

When you're waiting for something special, time slows down to a crawl. I could hardly wait for the fireworks.

Frita's daddy was holding a special prayer service that night to pray for our country, so he agreed to let Frita stay over at my house. Pop set up the tent and laid out our sleeping bags, and Frita came over extra early for dinner. We sat in the living room to watch TV and Pop didn't even get riled up because the news was all about the celebrations going on around the country. They showed the tall ships lining up in New York Harbor and a place called George in the state of Washington where they'd made a sixty-foot cherry pie. I was hard-pressed to say where I'd have rather been.

When dinner was ready, Momma called us in to eat. Usually Frita was the first one to the table because Momma made stuff Frita never got at her house, like macaroni and cheese from a box, and hot dogs boiled on the stove.

Tonight we were having spaghetti with salad and Wonder Bread. Momma even made blueberry pie for dessert so we'd have something red, something white, and something blue. But Frita didn't hardly seem to notice.

I wondered if she was thinking about Mr. Evans. I was real excited for her to cross him off her list, but when I asked if she was ready, Frita just shrugged. Then Momma had to ask her three times to pass the spaghetti. She was so un-Frita-Wilson-like it made me downright uncomfortable.

By the time we walked into town, I was getting a nervous feeling in my gut. Things were pressing in again.

When we arrived, the lawn in front of the town hall was full. There was a podium set up in the front all decorated with paper-bag lanterns and American flags, and the mayor was making a speech about the history of our country and the history of Hollowell. He kept talking about progress and how we'd made so much of it. I didn't pay attention. I was watching the people selling peanuts and flags.

"Want an American flag?" Pop asked me and Frita. Momma gave him the look that said *We ain't got the money for that,* but Pop leaned over and kissed her on the cheek.

"This occasion only comes once every two hundred years," he said, and then he bought two little flags with

*1776–1976* stitched on them—one for me and one for Frita. He also bought us each a bag of boiled peanuts.

"Go have some fun," he said, swatting me on the behind. "But come back for the fireworks. Momma and I will be right here..."

Me and Frita took off. We wove in and out of the crowd and ate our peanuts over by the Revolutionary War reenactment. Only Frita gave most of her peanuts to me.

"Don't you like 'em?" I asked.

"They're okay," she said, but she didn't sound like it.

We watched the guys dressed up in old uniforms pretending to be Redcoats and farmers. Then, when that was over, we listened to someone else making a speech, but that got boring.

"Think we should go find Mr. Evans?" I asked. We were sitting on the grass near the podium.

"In a bit," Frita said. She was pretending to be real interested in the speech.

"How 'bout now?" I asked a while later.

"Shush," Frita said. "Aren't you listening?"

I picked at some grass.

"It's getting darker," I said. "They're going to start the fireworks soon, and then how will you find him?"

Frita sighed. "I know where he is," she said, and she pointed to some men near the podium. Sure enough, there was Mr. Evans, Mr. Buselby, and Mr. Carmen standing in a clump, just like sixth-graders.

Me and Frita watched them for a while, then Frita stood up. She narrowed her eyes and jutted out her chin.

"Gabe," she said at last, "I'm going."

Then it was just like the rope swing. One minute Frita was standing next to me in the twilight, and the next minute she was walking straight toward Mr. Evans. I didn't know whether I ought to stay put or go with her, but suddenly I wondered if I hadn't thought things through. Maybe it was the way Mr. Evans and Mr. Carmen looked just like Duke and Frankie, or maybe it was the way Frita'd been acting all night, but I started to wonder if this was such a great idea after all. Except now it was too late.

I got up and walked closer, but I stopped a little ways away while Frita pushed her way in. She slid up next to Mr. Evans.

"Mr. Evans," I heard her say, and her voice sounded real little. At first no one noticed Frita. She stood there waiting, then she looked at me and shrugged. She had a real funny look on her face, and I got a weird feeling in the pit of my stomach—real sour, like before you get a stomachache. I motioned for her to come back.

"Forget it," I said, but the words didn't come out. I thought of my dream and the Mr. Evans spider waiting to pounce.

"Mr. Evans," Frita said again, and this time he looked down.

It was strange the way everything happened right then.

Mr. Evans looked at Frita, and then he said something to Mr. Carmen. Frita looked confused. My stomach was tightening and tightening and I wondered if I ought to run and get Pop, but I couldn't leave Frita. Then Mr. Evans smiled and leaned in like he was whispering something special to her.

That's when Frita's eyes went big as full moons and she took two steps backward real quick. She tripped over Mr. Evans's foot even though Frita never hardly trips. He laughed like it was funny, and all the other men laughed too. Then she was scrambling up and running toward me so fast, you would have thought there was a ghost on her heels.

"What happened?" I said when she got close, but Frita didn't stop. She kept right on going.

That's when the fireworks started—a few at first, then more and more. They were loud, cracking and popping over our heads, but Frita didn't look up. She went straight to my pop and stood next to him.

I mouthed the words *What did he say?* a hundred times, but Frita just shook her head. She took Pop's hand and squeezed it hard. Pop looked down, surprised, but I saw him squeeze back.

"Pretty amazing," he said, squatting down so he was nearer to us. "Don't you think?"

I hadn't even looked up yet.

"Look at that one!" Momma said, pointing up. She laughed and pulled me close. "Isn't it great to live in America?" she said, kissing the top of my head. "Just imagine—someday you'll tell your children you were alive for the Bicentennial!"

I looked over at Frita. "Yup," I said, "sure is great." But really I was thinking how no one better have said anything mean to my best friend.

Momma held me tight and Pop grinned up at the sky, and right then the biggest starburst of red, white, and blue exploded over our heads. The crowd said, "Oooh!" and "Aaah!" like it was magical, but Frita Wilson didn't make a sound.

# Chapter 19

# GHOST STORIES

IT WAS LATE BY THE TIME WE GOT HOME. WE WERE SUPPOSED TO sleep outside in the tent and stay awake until the sun came up, but Frita didn't say a word the whole walk back. I wasn't so keen on sleeping outdoors anymore, but the tent was already up and Pop had laid out our sleeping bags.

"Get all your stuff together before you go out to the tent," Momma said. "I don't want you kids running through the house all night. Don't forget your flashlights. And Gabe, make sure you use the bathroom this time—"

"Mom*ma*!"

Momma gave me that look that said, *Well, remember last time?* but I ignored her. Frita brushed her teeth like a robot, staring straight ahead. She spit out her toothpaste extra quick and went in the other room to get on her pajamas. Then we walked outdoors real solemn and zipped ourselves up inside the tent. We sat on our sleeping bags, and I looked at Frita. No one was talking, so I cleared my throat the way I'd seen Pop do when things got strained.

"So," I said at last, "what'd he say?"

Frita picked at a string on her sleeping bag. "Who?" she asked.

"Mr. Evans!" I practically yelled. "What'd he whisper?"

Frita's face went blank, like she had no idea what I was talking about.

"Oh, that," Frita said. "I couldn't hear him on account of all the noise. Too bad, huh?"

That was a lie and I knew it, but I nodded real slow. "Yup," I said. "Too bad."

Frita lay down on top of her sleeping bag and took out her flashlight.

"Let's have a flashlight war," she said. We pretended our light beams were swords and whooshed them all around. Frita won every time.

"Want to eat marshmallows?" I asked. Frita nodded, and we pulled out the bag Momma had given us to eat in the tent. We ate a whole bunch of them and they were good, but the fun was missing.

"Want to tell ghost stories?" I asked at last. "To celebrate how brave we are now?" Truth was, I wasn't so crazy about ghost stories, but Frita loved them.

"Umm, okay, I guess," Frita said. She reached up and tried to touch the top of the tent with her toes.

"Don't you want to?" I asked.

"I want to," Frita said. She'd stuck one leg so high in the air, it touched the top, then she let it fall with a whoosh onto her sleeping bag. She sat up and pulled her legs under her. "I'll go first, okay?" she said.

"Okay," I said, a little nervous. Frita seemed real serious.

"Want to hear a real one?" she asked.

I was sure I didn't, but I nodded anyway.

"Well," said Frita, "it has to do with the number-one thing on my list."

Now I sat up real straight. I turned my flashlight off so only Frita's flashlight was shining in the middle of the tent. Then I pulled my legs in cross-legged and leaned my elbows on my knees.

"Tell me," I whispered.

Frita leaned forward. Every now and then she'd glance at the zippered-up door of the tent just to make sure no one was out there.

"Well," she said in a whisper, "when me and Terrance were living in Alabama, and I was just a baby, Daddy and Momma were working with Martin Luther King to change the laws that kept black people segregated. There were lots of white people who didn't like this, and one night, some of them snuck onto our lawn. They were part of the Ku Klux Klan."

My eyes popped. "No!"

"Yup," Frita said. "Terrance told me all about it. Usually he won't talk about it none, but this one time I asked how come he's so angry at white people all the time, so he told me.

"He said it was an extra-hot night, just like this one, and Momma was rocking me to sleep. Daddy was helping Terrance with his reading when they heard a sound, like animals in the yard, so they went to see what it was. Daddy and Terrance were laughing about skunks, but when they opened the door, there was a ring of men all around our yard. They had on white sheets and pointy hats with only the eyeholes cut out, and they lit a cross on fire right outside our front door. Terrance said it smelled like ash and he couldn't breathe, staring at all those ghosts.

"One of them started calling Daddy bad names. He yelled, 'Come out and we'll let your family go,' and Terrance said right then Daddy's face crumpled like paper burning in a flame. That's exactly how he described it."

Frita's eyes were real serious.

All the spit had dried out of my mouth. "What happened? Did he go out?" I asked, but it was hardly a croak.

Frita shook her head. "Terrance said that's when Momma came flying down the stairs. She had me pressed to her chest, and she slammed that door shut and held on to Daddy real tight. Then she grabbed Terrance's arm so hard it hurt and dragged him into her bedroom. She made him climb into the clothes hamper even though he could barely fit in it. Then she handed me in.

" 'Promise,' she whispered to Terrance, 'that you won't come out until your daddy or I say it's all right. Promise you'll keep your sister silent. Promise,' Momma said. She said it over and over again until he'd promised lots of times. Then she and Daddy were gone so long, Terrance thought they were dead, and the whole time he sat in the clothes hamper and prayed. He prayed, 'Dear God, please keep Momma and Daddy safe,' and he whispered it in my ear like he was telling me a story, so I never made a sound."

I could feel my eyes brimming up. "Then what happened?" I asked.

"They stayed a long time," Frita said. "Then around one o'clock in the morning the cross burned out and those ghosts left our yard. The next day, Daddy got all the pastors from the different churches together—white and black—and they went to visit each of the people who'd been dressed up in the white sheets."

"What'd he do that for?" I asked. "How'd he know who they were if they were wearing sheets? What happened once they saw him?" All my questions were running into one another.

Frita held the flashlight tight.

"Daddy says everyone knows who's in the Ku Klux Klan. He says even though they keep themselves hidden, a man can't keep his views hidden in real life, and it's not hard to figure out who they really are."

"Wasn't he afraid?" I asked.

"Yes," said Frita, "but Daddy says he wanted everyone to know that he knew who they were. He said people will do things they wouldn't do otherwise if they think no one can see them. After that, he figured the Ku Klux Klan would either kill him or leave him be. I guess we were pretty lucky, because they let him be."

I could feel the sweat dripping down my neck and it wasn't just because it was hot out.

"We got the Ku Klux Klan around here, don't we?" I asked, even though I mostly knew the answer. But I didn't want to believe it.

Frita nodded. "I know for sure we do," she said.

"How do you know?" I asked, and Frita looked at me real steady.

"Because Mr. Evans told me so."

"He did?" I croaked.

Frita nodded. "Want to know what he said?"

This time I nodded.

"He said if me and you weren't careful, the Klan might pay us a visit someday."

I stood up so quick, my feet barely made it under me. "I'm telling Pop!" I said, but Frita's eyes went wide and she pulled so hard on my sleeve, I fell right back down again.

"Don't!" she said. "Your pop will tell my daddy and I'll get in trouble something fierce. Daddy told me I wasn't ever to go around men like Mr. Evans, and if he finds out, he'll be so mad . . ."

"But what if they come after us? What if they're out there dressing up right now?"

Frita glanced at the door of the tent. "They wouldn't," she said, but then she shivered. Then I shivered. Then I got to thinking how we were all alone. At night. Just me and Frita.

"You hear something?" I asked, and my voice got high and squeaky like it does when I get scared.

"No," said Frita, real quick. "Did you?"

"No," I said, but just at that moment I *did* hear something. Sounded like a twig snapping outside the tent. I looked at Frita and I could tell from her face she'd heard it too. We sat real still.

"What was that?" Frita whispered so soft, I could barely hear.

"I don't know," I whispered back, but my mind sure thought it knew. I was picturing a whole line of white ghosts coming out of the woods. Maybe they were sneaking around the tent this very minute, waiting to grab us.

Frita grabbed my hand and she squeezed so tight, I thought she might squeeze it straight off.

"What are we going to do?" Frita asked, and I knew she was picturing exactly what I was picturing. And she was asking *me* what to do.

"Think my momma and pop would hear us if we screamed?"

Frita looked like she might cry. "I don't know," she said, shaking her head. She squeezed my hand again and this time I squeezed back real tight.

"They will," I said, making up my mind. "Momma hears everything, and Pop is a real good fighter. I promise I won't let go of you, no matter what."

"Okay," Frita whispered. "On the count of three. One . . . two . . ."

We screamed louder than we'd ever screamed before. We both stood up at once and started to run, only we forgot to unzip the tent. Since I'd promised I wouldn't let go of Frita's hand, we both had only one hand to work with and we sure couldn't get that zipper unzipped. The whole tent fell down on top of us, only it felt like maybe someone pushed it down. We kept screaming and running and pulling that tent along with us even though we couldn't see which way we were headed. We were just one big bundle of tent and scream-ing people.

Then two huge arms were coming down over us and I thought we were goners until I heard Pop's voice shouting above all our screaming.

It took a long, long time, but finally Pop got that zipper undone and me and Frita tumbled out. I still wasn't letting go of her hand and she still wasn't letting go of mine, and we were both trying to talk at the same time, only neither of us had any breath left from all the screaming. I looked around, wondering how many Ku Klux Klan people were there, but the yard was empty. Pop was in his pajamas and Momma was in her nightgown with her hair curlers in. They looked tired and wide-awake all at the same time.

"What's wrong?" Pop kept asking. "What happened?"

Once I looked around and saw there weren't any Ku Klux Klan guys waiting, I thought Momma and Pop would be mad for sure. We'd woken them up and knocked down the tent, and all the neighbor's lights were on. But they didn't get mad.

Pop was holding Frita by the shoulders, and Frita was holding my hand tight. Then she started choking out the whole story even though she'd said she wasn't going to tell. She told Pop all about the Ku Klux Klan and what happened to her daddy and about Mr. Evans and how we thought there might be Klan people outside the tent and just like that, without a lick of warning, Pop's eyes overflowed.

Never in my entire life had I seen Pop cry, but he grabbed Frita up like she was his own child and he held her tight and kissed the top of her head. He kept whispering, *"child, child,"* like there was nothing else to say. And the funny thing was, Frita didn't seem to mind. My best friend, Frita, who was supposed to be almost liberated from all her fears, let my pop rock her back and forth like she was a little, little kid.

# Chapter 20

# A NEW PLAN

IT WAS STRANGE HOW THE SUMMER SEEMED TO END THAT NIGHT EVEN though it was only the Fourth of July. Me and Frita slept inside for the rest of the night, and in the morning Pop called the Wilsons and they came over and sat around our little kitchen table to discuss the whole thing. Even Terrance came, and he'd never been to my trailer before. Not even once.

"I just don't understand why you spoke to Mr. Evans in the first place," Mr. Wilson said, looking hard at Frita. "You *know* better . . ."

I'd never felt so bad in my entire life.

"I talked her into it," I said. "Because I used to be scared of Terrance, but after we talked, I wasn't so scared anymore."

Terrance shook his head. "It's not your fault, Twerp."

Then Frita said, "I knew I shouldn't have done it."

Her momma said, "No, you shouldn't have," but she sighed like she was tired instead of mad. "Something ought to be done," she muttered, studying her empty coffee cup.

Pop got up and poured some more. "Not much to be done

about the Klan," he said. "Can't stop them from existing. Maybe there are some things people *ought* to be afraid of."

That sounded right to me, but Mr. Wilson frowned.

"There's always something to be done," he said, looking from me to Frita and Terrance. "We just need some Peace Warriors to stand up to them. Isn't that right, kids?"

Pop gave me a real curious look, but Mr. Wilson kept talking.

"When a grown man threatens a little girl," he said, "he does it because he thinks he can get away with it. He thinks that little girl will be too scared to do anything about it, and that everyone she tells will be just as scared. Only this time he picked the wrong little girl."

Frita sat up straight. "That's right," she said, "because me and Gabe have been getting brave all summer. Gabe's practicing for the fifth grade."

Terrance snorted, but Mrs. Wilson gave him a look, so he kept his mouth shut. I glanced over at Momma, but she just looked worried.

"What do you think we should do?" she asked.

"Let's storm their trailer," Terrance said. "No one's going to threaten my little sister."

Mrs. Wilson scowled. "What would that accomplish?" she asked, one hand on her hip. "Then they'd storm our house and we'd have to fight back . . ."

"Well, we can't just hide out," Terrance said. His hands

were balling up into fists, but Mrs. Wilson rested her hand on his arm.

"That's not what I'm suggesting," she said, turning to the rest of us. "How about this. Mr. Wilson is preaching at a rally in Hollowell for Jimmy Carter at the beginning of August. He could say something then. We could gather all of our friends and neighbors and ask them to stand with us to remind people that America is about freedom for everyone. Not just white people. We'd be sending a strong message to Carl Evans and anyone else in the Ku Klux Klan."

Mr. Wilson nodded in agreement. "No one's going to hide from this," he said, looking at Terrance. "Not this time."

Momma took a deep breath. "I don't know . . . ," she said, but Mr. Wilson smiled real gentle.

"I know you're afraid," he told Momma, "But if there's one thing I've learned it's that people will do anything if they think no one's going to stand up to them. As soon as they've got a crowd against them, they're not so brave."

Momma looked over at Pop, but he was swirling the coffee in his coffee cup.

"How would they get the message?" Pop asked. "They're certainly not going to come to the rally."

"Actually," Mrs. Wilson said, "there's almost always someone who shows up from the other side. They don't make themselves known, mind you, but they show up. It's human nature to be curious. Regardless," she added, "they'll hear about it. People talk and the newspaper will cover the story.

We might even get on TV if we have a large enough turnout or if Jimmy Carter shows up."

"You sure we won't be stirring up trouble?" Momma asked. "It's not like Mr. Evans did anything, and we can't prove he's in the Klan. Maybe he just said that to scare Frita."

"Isn't that enough?" Terrance asked.

For once no one corrected him.

Mrs. Wilson took Momma's hand. "If someone wants to take our children's security away from them, don't you think we should do something about it?"

That's when I remembered Pop's words from the day at the catfish pond.

*Do you want to let someone take something from you that you can never get back again?*

Pop looked at me like he was thinking the same thing, then he nodded real slow. "You're right," he said at last. "What can I do?"

Mr. Wilson grinned just like Frita. "You could stand up with me when I give that speech," he said. "Maybe say a few words to the crowd."

Pop's eyes went wide. I knew he'd meant what could he do with his hands—like building signs or platforms. He glanced at Momma. "I'm not exactly . . . I mean, I'm not so sure what I'd say is all, and . . ."

It was the first time I'd ever seen Pop look scared.

"Pop! You could tell that story about Jimmy Carter," I said. "The one you told me."

"That's perfect," Mr. Wilson said. "Gabe told me all about it."

He winked, and Frita hopped up and down.

"What about me and Gabe?" she asked. "What can we do?"

This time all the adults answered at once.

"You can stay out of trouble!"

Even Terrance nodded like he agreed.

Frita told me later that meant they were *uuu*-nanimous.

# Chapter 21

# THE LAST OF THE LISTS

IF SIGNS AND PORTENTS WERE TRUE, THEN MY DREAM REALLY WAS one, because Mr. Evans's words were like the sticky strands of a spiderweb. Even though they seemed tiny, we knew they could spread everywhere until we were caught and couldn't get out. Look how they'd spread so far. First, he'd called Frita a nigger and only my pop had stood up to him, so he'd kept right on going, and now the whole town of Hollowell was getting involved because Mr. Wilson was going door-to-door asking everyone to come to the rally.

Me and Frita walked into town one afternoon about two weeks after the Bicentennial, and even though we were trying hard to stay out of things, that wasn't easy to do. We were getting ice cream cones at the general store and everyone we met had something to say.

*"Did Carl Evans really say that to you?"*

*"How come you kids are stirring up trouble?"*

*"Who could believe it? In 1976!"*

Frita was real polite, but I could tell she was tired of listening to them.

"Let's walk down the old dirt road," she said once we'd

eaten our ice cream. I waited for the familiar twist in my stomach, but this time it didn't come.

"Okay," I said. Me and Frita turned off Main Street and started walking. We walked real slow and I didn't even listen for eighteen-wheelers or check to see if the cows were loose.

"Want to go on the rope swing?" I asked after a while, but Frita didn't have her swimsuit.

"Want to build a tree fort?" she suggested.

"Nah. Too hot."

"Want to finish our lists?" Frita asked.

We hadn't talked about our lists since the fireworks.

I shrugged. Truth was, I'd been thinking on things. I'd come to a decision a week ago and the only reason I hadn't said anything was because I was gathering my courage.

I opened my mouth, but it was all dried up.

"Frita," I said at last, "I don't think it's working."

Frita stopped walking. "What's not working?"

"The lists," I said. I thought about what she'd said that day I squished the centipede. "You were right. I'm not getting any braver. Guess I'm one of the chicken ones."

"That's not true," Frita said. "I was just mad when I said that. You've gotten lots braver. You've jumped off the rope swing a bunch of times and you kept Jimmy all summer."

"Yeah," I said, "but those aren't the ones that counted. I'm still plenty scared of the fifth grade. I've thought it over and I'm staying behind, no matter what."

Frita's face fell. "But you said you wouldn't be scared of mean teachers anymore, and we planned out what you'd do if you got locked in the toilet again . . ."

I drew pictures in the sand with my foot.

"But I'm twice as scared of Duke," I said at last. "I've had two bad dreams where he was burning stuff on the playground and yelling for you to come out. What if he does something real bad?"

"He won't," said Frita. "Duke is a scaredy-cat. Besides, we're having the rally, remember? You won't be scared of him after that. We're gonna stand up to those Evans's—me and you, our mommas and daddys, and Terrance . . ."

Frita was on a roll, but she might as well have been talking to herself because it wasn't going to make any difference. All I could hear was Duke's voice in my head.

*"No one's going to clap for Frita Wilson if I can help it."*

All this time I'd thought he hated Frita because she could pummel him, but now I knew different. Now I knew what real hate was, and it was the scariest thing of all, even if I hadn't put it on my list.

I shook my head. "I made up my mind," I said. "And you got to stay back with me because you pinky-swore it."

Frita's face fell. I suspect she'd forgotten all about that.

"Gabe," she said, her lip quivering. "I can't. Momma and Daddy would never let me, and I don't even want to. You got to move up with me. *You got to!*"

"Nope," I said. "I won't. No one can make me." Then I corrected myself. "No one can make *us*, I mean."

But Frita shook her head. She looked sadder than I'd ever seen her.

"I won't stay back," she said at last. She looked at me real hard. "Guess you'll have to learn to be brave without me."

I could hardly believe it. Now we'd both broken a pinky swear.

We stood face-to-face on the old dirt road. Then Frita turned in the opposite direction.

"Guess I better go," she said. "Momma will probably be calling me in for dinner soon."

It was hours yet before dinner, but I shrugged. I couldn't decide whether I was mad or sad or just plain terrified.

"Okay," I said at last.

Frita got set up to run, but she looked back over her shoulder.

"Call me when you find your courage," she told me. "Then we'll move up together, okay?"

I didn't say a word. I knew she wanted me to say "All right," like I'd change my mind and everything would go back to normal, but I didn't *want* to change my mind. I wanted Frita to change hers.

Frita waited a long time, but I didn't say anything, so she took off.

"See ya, Gabriel King," she said. I watched her run until

she was a tiny speck in the distance, and soon as she was gone, I missed her something terrible.

"See ya," I hollered at last, loud as I could. My eyes were brimming over and I waved super hard and whistled my extra-loud whistle, but it was too late.

I knew she couldn't hear me.

# Chapter 22

# READY FOR THE RALLY

EVERY DAY AFTER THAT, I STOOD NEXT TO THE TELEPHONE WITH MY hand on the receiver, but I never did call Frita. I thought about all the liberatin' me and Frita had done over the summer and I wished it had made a difference, but I still didn't want to go to the fifth grade.

Maybe Frita would change her mind. Or maybe she'd be better off without me. We'd *both* broken our pinky swears thanks to Duke, so who knew what else could happen.

I had a real bad feeling in my stomach and it only got worse as the rally got closer. Pop, Terrance, and Mr. and Mrs. Wilson sat in the living room almost every night, but Frita didn't come with them. She stayed with her great-aunt Alma even though she and Frita hardly got along.

I listened to our families planning everything out.

*"We've got permission to use the elementary school. We'll set up in the back where the kids had their Moving-Up Day."*

*"How's that speech coming, Allen?"*

*"Terrance, you take the Peace Warriors out knocking on doors. Make sure folks are coming."*

It was all business. I sat outside on the front steps, wishing Frita was here. Sometimes Momma would bring out lemonade and we'd sit side by side, real quiet.

"You and Frita in a fight?" she asked me once, but I just shrugged. Wasn't exactly a fight. I wasn't sure what it was.

Momma kissed me on the head.

"These things happen," she told me. "You'll get past it. Right now Frita's busy helping her daddy get ready for the rally. She probably just needs a little time on her own. Soon as this settles down, you'll be best buddies again."

But Momma didn't know everything. Soon as this settled down, it would be time for school and I'd have to make my decision once and for all.

I thought I might talk to Pop about it, but he was too busy practicing his speech.

Seemed like all he did now was read it in the mirror and change stuff he'd already written. I'd say, "Want to sit on the steps before the Wilsons get here?" and he'd say, "Not right now, I've got to fix this paragraph." I thought we might watch the news together and get all riled up about politics, but the only politics Pop was interested in were the ones right here in Hollowell.

I finally settled on talking to the cows. I'd gotten real friendly with the cow who swatted her ear at me. Even though she didn't say much, she was a decent listener.

I walked down to the old dirt road one night after dinner and planted myself next to the cotton field. Sun was setting and the sky was pink and it was starting to smell like August.

"I sure miss Frita," I told the cow. "There's no one to make obstacle courses with, or to ride bikes with. Nobody walks into town with me or jumps off the rope swing." I paused. "Life sure is plain."

The wind blew through the cotton, rustling the stalks.

"Think I should just go to the fifth grade?" I asked.

The cow's tail swished back and forth.

"But what if something happens? What if Duke does something mean?"

I thought of a hundred horrible things that could happen.

"What if he's mad about the rally and takes it out on us? Frita will need to watch out for herself, don't you think?"

I studied the cow's face real careful to see what she was thinking, but her eyelids just drooped and she chewed on a patch of grass.

"Fine," I said, lying back in the cotton, "that's easy for you to say. You're a cow. But I'm a chicken. A body can't just stop being a chicken."

I waited for the cow to argue with me. Maybe she'd say, "You can do it, Gabriel King. You just got to have faith." But that cow didn't say anything, and after that neither did I.

Things couldn't be good when you were talking to a cow.

Sometimes I wonder what might have happened if it hadn't been for Terrance.

Well, Terrance and Pop, I mean.

It was the night before the rally and the Wilsons were over at my trailer again, going over the final details with Momma and Pop. I'd taken to sitting outside with Jimmy while they talked. Partly because it made my stomach feel funny to think about everything that was going to happen, but mostly because I couldn't stand to see the Wilsons without Frita. Mr. and Mrs. Wilson never said a word, but I knew they were wondering how come Frita had suddenly taken a liking to Great-aunt Alma.

That night, I was sitting outside in my overalls with my bare feet tickling the grass, trying to catch a cricket for Jimmy's dinner, when the front door slammed open. Momma and Pop never slammed the door and it was way too early for the Wilsons to be leaving, so I looked up.

There was Terrance, standing on my front step.

He sure looked tall, staring down at me. His legs were solid like tree trunks and his afro was all puffed out around his head. He had on a T-shirt that said POWER TO THE PEOPLE and for a minute I felt scared of him, just like I used to. But then he sat down beside me and he was just Terrance again, Frita's big brother who made pounding fun.

"What're you doing, Twerp?" Terrance asked.

I put the cover back on Jimmy's tank. "Nothin'."

"What's up with you and Frito?"

I didn't expect that question because everyone else was tiptoeing around the subject, but I guess Terrance wasn't like everyone else.

I shrugged. "She doesn't want to see me."

Terrance snorted. "Well, that ain't true," he said. "She couldn't get more miserable if she tried. Moping around the house all week. Always hanging around the basement. Driving me crazy."

He sounded real annoyed, but only partway. I sat up just a little bit.

"Really?" I asked, but Terrance just scowled.

"Listen," he said, "I've got something to tell you. I've made up my mind. I'm moving to Atlanta soon as this rally is over."

My grin faded. "Atlanta?"

"Yup," he said. "I'm going to live with my uncle Rory and get a job in the city."

"Doing what?" I asked.

But this time it was Terrance who shrugged.

"Who knows," he said, "but I can't wait around here my whole life. Sometimes you've got to take a chance." He looked at me real steady, then he reached into his pocket. "I got something for you," he said. "And it's important, so you better pay attention."

Terrance took out a crumpled piece of paper and pressed it hard into my palm. Then he closed my fingers around it into a fist. He held them closed tight just for a minute.

"You wouldn't have been my first choice for Frito's best friend," he said, "but you're okay. You've got potential. Just don't screw it up."

Then Terrance let go and stood up.

"See you at the rally, Twerp."

He disappeared back inside the house and I stared at the paper in my fist. Terrance had never given me anything before and I couldn't imagine what it was. One by one I peeled away my fingers, then I smoothed out the paper. On it was Frita's handwriting.

My Fear List
Frita Wilson

1. Ku Klux Klan
2. Mr. Evans
3. ~~rope swing~~
4. kissing
5. ~~roller skating on the yellow line~~
6. ~~brussels sprouts~~
7. ~~the Evans trailer~~
8. dying
9. Terrance leaving home
10. not having Gabe with me in the fifth grade

I stared at that paper so long, I thought my eyes might weld themselves to it. I'd never seen Frita's whole list before. I wondered where Terrance had gotten it, but from the looks of things he'd pulled it out of the trash. I read it over and over again, but mostly I read the last two. *Terrance leaving home* and *not having Gabe with me in the fifth grade.*

Maybe Frita really did need me.

I was still sitting there staring when the Wilsons left for the night. Terrance didn't even look at me. He just climbed in the car and started the engine while Mr. and Mrs. Wilson said their good-byes.

"See you tomorrow, Gabe," Mrs. Wilson said, ruffling my hair as she walked by.

"That's right," said Mr. Wilson, "tomorrow's the big day. Frita sure will be excited to see you."

They were being extra nice, but I hardly noticed. All I could think about was Frita's list. I listened to the rumble of their car driving away, but I still didn't get up. I stayed out there until it got dark. Then I folded the list and put it in my pocket. I stood outside my front door, watching the way the light from inside spilled out onto the steps. I could hear Momma and Pop's voices carrying softly.

Part of me wanted to stand there forever, but part of me knew it was time to go in.

I walked inside and let the front door shut with a snap. Pop was standing in the living room in his fancy clothes.

"Do you think I should wear this striped tie?" he was asking Momma.

She gave him that look that said *Quit asking me*, because Pop had probably asked a million times already and it was the only tie he owned so he pretty much had to wear it no matter what. Pop held the tie up to his shirt and turned from side to side. I missed his work pants and clompy old work boots. I bet he missed them too because he looked real uncomfortable.

"I don't know," he said, itching his collar. "It's old and it sure doesn't go with this shirt. I bet the other men will be dressed nice. I heard the mayor's going to be there and TV crews . . ."

I put Jimmy's tank on the counter and Pop studied his reflection in the glass.

"What do you think, Jimmy?" he asked, leaning in. "Think Gabe's pop is going to make a fool out of himself?"

Momma sighed. She glanced at me and I waited for her to say something encouraging, but she slipped out of the room instead. I thought about how nervous Pop was, and for the first time ever I realized maybe *he* needed me too.

"You'll be great, Pop," I said. "Just like Jimmy Carter."

Pop sighed and set down the tie. "Maybe I should stay home," he said. "There will be plenty of speeches without mine. Who needs another speech?"

I'd heard Pop's speech so many times, I could practically recite it myself, but it was a darn good one. Made me feel braver every time. I tried to think how I'd explain that to Pop, but it turns out I didn't have to, because Momma slid up behind him. She reached around his waist and handed him a long, thin box with a gold bow on it.

"I wasn't going to give it to you until tomorrow," she said. Then she laughed. Finally, she had to say, "Open it."

Pop fumbled with the fancy bow, but Momma leaned her

chin on his shoulder and waited real patient while he pulled off the top. I stood on my tiptoes to see inside. It was a brand-new tie with a shiny golden tie clip. Nicer than any tie I'd ever seen. Pop stared at Momma like he couldn't believe it.

"We don't have the money for this," he said, but Momma's face was soft, like she knew he was going to say that.

"I saved up," she said. "I put aside a little of the grocery money every week. You're going to look so handsome on that stage." She kissed Pop on the cheek.

"It's real nice," Pop said, his eyes glistening. He set the tie in the box extra careful, then he swung Momma up like they were dancing. For the first time since the Bicentennial, he laughed.

"Gabe," he said, "put on some music."

I climbed over the couch and turned on the record player and the music came on real loud, but no one said to turn it down. Instead, Pop dipped Momma low.

"Who's afraid of a silly speech?" he said, loud above the music. He twirled her around the living room.

"Who's afraid of being a fool?"

Momma laughed, and her face glowed like a full moon.

"Who's afraid of the Ku Klux Klan?" Pop asked, and me and Momma both yelled, "Not us!"

Then Pop picked me up and we all three twirled around until we fell on the couch. We lay there laughing and listening to the music fill up our trailer.

"Everything's going to be all right," Pop said at last. And

finally I knew he was right. Then he said something I won't ever forget.

"Ain't nothing so scary when you've got people you love," Pop said.

Right then I knew I'd found my courage.

It was like a lock found its key and sprung open.

All this time I'd been trying not to be scared, and it turns out all I had to do was be brave. Wasn't nothing going to keep fifth grade from being scary, but there wasn't nothing going to keep me from my best friend neither. That's what being brave was all about.

# Chapter 23

# AIN'T NOTHING SO SCARY . . .

THE NEXT MORNING, I GOT UP AND DRESSED FAST AS I'D EVER DONE it. When I got out to the kitchen, Pop was putting on his brand-new tie. Boy, did he look sharp.

"Mr. Wilson called," he was saying to Momma. "There's a rumor floating around that Jimmy Carter himself is coming to the rally. They're expecting an overflow crowd." Pop looked at me. "Don't get your hopes up," he said, "but he is home in Plains, which isn't too far from here."

I rubbed my eyes. Jimmy Carter? Coming to our rally?

That seemed near to impossible, but after this summer, who knew what could happen.

"We got to go right now," I said, stuffing down my toast and tugging on Pop's sleeve.

"I said not to get your hopes up," Pop reminded me, but it wasn't Jimmy Carter I couldn't wait to see. It was Frita Wilson.

Me, Momma, and Pop took the truck to the elementary school where they were setting up, and was it ever crowded. Looked like the crowd at the Bicentennial, only this time we'd be making our own fireworks.

"Come on," Momma said, taking my hand and Pop's hand in hers. "Let's find the Wilsons."

We went out back to the school yard. At first I couldn't see Frita in the crowd, but then I spotted her. She was standing up front with her daddy and she sure looked pretty. Her hair was done up with bows and she was smiling huge at all the adults. Her momma motioned us over.

"This is Mr. and Mrs. King," Mrs. Wilson said to the others when we got close. "They're Gabriel's parents."

Then Momma and Pop were shaking hands and saying hello and it didn't matter that we lived in the smallest trailer in the Hollowell Trailer Park. They looked just like real politicians.

*Huh,* I thought. *Guess that's how a peanut farmer got to run for president of the United States.*

I tugged on Frita's sleeve.

"Hey," I said, "I got to tell you something."

Frita's eyes looked hopeful. "What is it?" she asked, but I didn't want to tell her with all the adults around.

"Want to sit under the picnic table?"

Frita thought it over.

"I guess so," she said. "For a minute."

We wove in and out of the crowd until we found our table, but this time we didn't crawl underneath like we usually did. We sat on top and swung our legs down.

"Frita," I said at last, "I changed my mind."

"About what?" she asked, even though I suspected she knew.

"The fifth grade," I said. "I'm going."

Frita's face split into a grin.

"For real?"

"Pinky sw . . ." I stopped. "Cross my heart and spit on the ground."

Then I did it so Frita would know I meant it for real. She swung her feet and studied me real good.

"Gabe," she asked, "what finally made you brave?"

I knew the answer, but I wasn't sure how to explain it, so I just shrugged. "You did."

" 'Cause of the liberating?"

"Sort of."

Frita grinned again, and we sat quiet, just me and her, and I thought how this really was the best summer ever.

"Frita Wilson," I said, "you're my best friend."

Frita looked at me and I knew she meant it back, but she didn't get a chance to say it because the microphones screeched in the distance. Mr. Wilson was asking everyone to sit down.

Frita hopped off the picnic table.

"Come on," she said. "Terrance is saving me a seat on the bleachers. Top row. Want to come?"

There was a time when the top row of the bleachers would've been on my list if I'd thought of it, but I hopped down. "Yup," I said.

We could hear Mr. Wilson introducing all the people who would be speaking at the rally.

*"Mayor Roberts, Reverend Jordan, Allen King . . ."*

I listened to the crowd clapping for Pop and I was real proud. I bet he was nervous up there on the stage, but he was doing it anyway, just like me and the fifth grade. I let loose one of my super-duper whistles. Then me and Frita got ready to make a beeline for the bleachers, only that's when we got waylaid one last time.

I don't know what made me turn around and look under the farthest picnic table at the edge of the school yard. Maybe it was because I suspected me and Frita wouldn't come here to hide out anymore after this, not when we'd be West Wing fifth-graders. I wanted to take one last look at what had been our spot. Only this time I saw something I hadn't counted on.

Way in the back, under the picnic table closest to the school building, there were two people hiding out. I could see them clearly even though they were far away.

I poked Frita in the ribs. "Look," I said.

There were Duke and Frankie. For a minute, my heart beat fast, just like it always did. But then I realized which of us was hiding out and which of us had most of Rockford and Hollowell behind them. I remembered what Mrs. Wilson had said about people coming to the rally to report back. I don't know how I knew it, but right then I was one hundred percent certain that Mr. Evans and Mr. Carmen were nowhere nearby. They'd put Duke and Frankie up to coming here instead, and that struck me as extra chicken.

I looked at Frita and Frita looked at me, and I knew we were thinking the exact same thing. We could get Duke and Frankie in some trouble if we wanted to. All we'd have to do was tell Terrance they were here, or maybe scream or yell for an adult. Frita could even whup them herself if she wanted to, but that's not what we did.

"Ready to go?" Frita asked.

"Yup," I said. "You think Jimmy Carter will show up today?"

"Maybe," said Frita. "But either way, it sure is a good crowd. I think just about everyone in Hollowell *and* Rockford showed up." She grinned and looked back at Duke and Frankie. "That'll show any Evans to call me a nigger," she said, and I thought, Yup, that was some true. You did not mess with Frita Wilson.

Frita got set to run. "Race ya."

Then me and her took off in a cloud of dust and I imagined what our feet must look like to Duke and Frankie watching us from way back under the picnic table. For a minute I almost felt sorry for them stuck under there, hiding out.

Then I was running fast, climbing the bleachers, and Terrance was making his friends squish over so me and Frita could squeeze in. Then Mr. Wilson was introducing my pop for real and he was standing up there in his brand-new tie with the shiny tie clip, and I was standing up to wave at him so he would remember that there ain't nothing so scary when you've got someone you love.

That's when I thought about Duke and Frankie one last time, and this time I didn't feel scared or mad or sorry for them. I hoped that maybe someday someone would liberate them too. Then maybe they'd figure out what love and courage were all about, and life would spring open like a lock that found its key.

What I'm Afraid Of
By Gabriel King

1. fifth grade
2. Duke Evans
3. Frankie Carmen
4. spiders
5. aligators
6. Terrance
7. loosing Momma or Pop
8. Fritas basement
9. earwig pinchers
10. loose cows
11. getting lost in the swamp
12. swinging off the rope swing
13. mising the school bus
14. big trucks and mean truck drivers
15. falling into the toilet
16. robbers
17. teachers who yell a lot
18. sentipedes
19. the old dirt road
20. getting eaten by buzards
21. the Evans trailer
22. ghosts
23. Frita being mad at me

24. clumps of sixth graders
25. getting my hand chopped off in momma's new blender
26. being pounded
27. roller skating on the hiway like on that TV show
28. calling a teacher momma by axident
29. never getting any taller
30. finding a worm in my sanwich
31. being locked in the bathroom at school
32. not being picked for gym teams
33. killer robots
34. falling off a high branch of a pecan tree
35. corpses
36. tornados
37. wars like Vietnam
38. raccoons, especially when they sound like bears outside your tent

## ACKNOWLEDGMENTS

So many people lent their time and talents to this book. First and foremost, I'd like to thank my editor, Kathy Dawson, for her hard work and vision. Her insight has been invaluable. I'd also like to thank my agent, Ginger Knowlton, who is the friend and advocate every writer dreams of.

My parents, William and Linda Going, are my best readers. My dad provided his expertise on spiders, catfish, and all things biological. He also accompanied me on a trip to Plains, Georgia, and read every draft of this book, even when I told him not to. Thanks to my mom for sharing her understanding of the children's book market, and for her instincts about what makes a great read.

Thank you to Dustin Adams for his unwavering support and for lending me his considerable writing talents as he critiqued draft after draft with patience and skill. Brenda Zook Friesen and Tobin Miller Shearer provided valuable anti-racist feedback. I'm also indebted to the St. Thomas community and The People's Institute for Survival and Beyond for prior anti-racist training. Thanks to Bob Strangfeld for sharing his historical knowledge and documents relating to 1976. I am grateful to Laura Blake Peterson, Elizabeth Gold, Susie and Laura Haldeman, Sara Sheiner, Zachary Miller Shearer, Tasha Toney-Thomas, and all those who read and commented on early drafts of this book. Thanks to Nicole Kasprzak and Nathan Bransford for their work behind the scenes.

Last but not least, thank you to Carol Daley for her work on the website and to April and Ben's Simple Things Bake Stand for providing the nourishment necessary to complete a novel (i.e.: fabulous cookies and baked goods).

# Literature Circle Questions

Use the questions and activities that follow to get more out of reading *The Liberation of Gabriel King* by K. L. Going.

1. Why doesn't Gabe make it to his own Moving-Up Day ceremony?

2. What is Gabe's number one fear?

3. Describe the nightmare that Gabe has the night after he catches Jimmy, his new pet spider.

4. Why do you think Gabe is so afraid of Frita's big brother Terrance?

5. At the Bicentennial celebration, why does Gabe suspect that Mr. Evans has said something cruel to Frita?

6. After a triumphant experience with the rope swing at the catfish pond, Gabe reflects: "There's nothing like success to boost your confidence." (page 94) Write about a time in your life when you felt more confident because you succeeded at something.

7. In chapter 19, Gabe learns about an episode from the Wilson family's past. How does this information help explain Frita's fears and Terrance's anger?

8. In the course of the story, how does Terrance change his attitude toward Gabe, and what do you think causes this change?

9. What most surprises Gabe when he sees Frita's fear list for the first time? Why is this an important discovery for him?

10. The night before the big rally, Gabe realizes how he can have courage in a frightening situation. In your own words, explain what Gabe learns about courage.

11. At the Bicentennial celebration, Frita refuses to talk after her run-in with Mr. Evans. What do you imagine she is thinking and feeling as she stands silently watching the fireworks?

12. Mr. Wilson explains the concept of "oppression" to Gabe: "Oppression is when you're put down. . . . It's when you don't have the freedom to be who you want to be because someone else doesn't believe you should

have that freedom." (page 102) Which characters in this book face oppression, and what kind of oppression do they experience?

13. In chapter 8, Frita tells Gabe that he should name his new pet spider: "Once you name him, you'll feel like he's yours and then you won't be scared of him anymore." (page 46) Explain in your own words what Frita is trying to accomplish with this advice.

14. In the quest to conquer his fears, Gabe takes several risks that he feels are quite dangerous. Make a list of all Gabe's adventures from the summer and rank them in order from most dangerous to least dangerous. In your opinion, are any of Gabe's fears appropriate?

15. How is the summer of 1976 a turning point in the lives of both Gabe and Frita? When they are older, what do you think each will remember most about this exciting summer?

*Note: These literature circle questions are keyed to Bloom's Taxonomy as follows: Knowledge: 1–3; Comprehension: 4–5; Application: 6–7; Analysis: 8–10; Synthesis: 11–13; Evaluation: 14–15.*

# Activities

1. What do you remember about your childhood fears? Think back to when you were a young child and create a list of your top ten fears at that time. Write an essay in which you describe your memories of your childhood fears and how they affected you. If you can, explain how you were able to overcome your fears.

2. During the summer of 1976, Gabe experiences success and failure, thrills and disappointments. Review the novel by listing the major events of Gabe's summer and create a line graph plotting the high and low points for Gabe. For each of the events on your line graph, draw a symbol or picture to represent the event and write a one-sentence description of what the event meant to Gabe.

3. *The Liberation of Gabriel King* addresses some historical events from the 1970s: the Watergate scandal, the election of Jimmy Carter, and the Bicentennial celebration. Find an adult who remembers one of these events well and interview him or her to learn more about the topic. Write a report on what you learn and be prepared to share it with your classmates.